What I Saw and How I Lied

What
I Saw
and How
I Lied

by Judy Blundell

SCHOLASTIC INC.

NEW YORK TORONTO LONDON AUCKLAND
SYDNEY MEXICO CITY NEW DELHI HONG KONG

This book is dedicated to
Betsy, Julie, and Katherine,
tall in their saddles

This book was originally published in hardcover by Scholastic Press in 2008.

ISBN: 978-0-439-90348-6

Copyright © 2008 by Judy Blundell.
All rights reserved. Published by Scholastic Inc.
SCHOLASTIC, SCHOLASTIC PRESS, and associated logos
are trademarks and/or registered trademarks of Scholastic Inc.

12 11 10 9 8 7 6 5 4 3 2 1   10 11 12 13 14 15/0

Printed in the U.S.A.   40
First Scholastic paperback printing, January 2010

The text for this book was set in Adobe Caslon Pro.
Book design by Elizabeth B. Parisi

Chapter 1

The match snapped, then sizzled, and I woke up fast. I heard my mother inhale as she took a long pull on a cigarette. Her lips stuck on the filter, so I knew she was still wearing lipstick. She'd been up all night.

She lay on the bed next to me. I felt her fingers on my hair and I kept sleep-breathing. I risked a look under my eyelashes.

She was in her pink nightgown, ankles crossed, head flung back against the pillows. Arm in the air, elbow bent, cigarette glowing in her fingers. Tanned legs glistening in the darkness. Blond hair tumbling past her shoulders.

I breathed in smoke and My Sin perfume. It was her smell. It filled the air.

I didn't move, but I could tell she knew I was awake. I kept on pretending to be asleep. She pretended not to know.

I breathed in and out, perfume and smoke, perfume and smoke, and we lay like that for a long time, until I heard the seagulls crying, sadder than a funeral, and I knew it was almost morning.

We never went to the hotel dining room now. They knew who we were; they'd seen our pictures in the paper. We knew they'd be saying, *Look at them eating toast — how can they be so heartless?*

I rode a bike down to the beach instead. In the basket I had a bottle of cream soda and two Baby Ruths. Breakfast.

The sky was full of stacked gray clouds and the air tasted like a nickel. The sun hadn't had time to bake the wetness from the sand. I had the place to myself. Me and the fishermen. Peter and I had watched them surf-casting together. One day, one of them had brought him home.

When Alice fell down the rabbit hole, she fell slow. She had time to notice things on her way down — *Oh, there's a teacup! There's a table!* So things seemed almost normal to her while she was falling. Then she bumped down and rolled into Wonderland, and all hell broke loose.

I'd noticed things on the way down, too. I'd seen it all — the way he took off his hat, the way he lit her cigarette, the way she walked away, her scarf trailing in her hand. Flower petals and a pineapple vase.

Now I had to look at it again. This time without me in it, wanting things to go my way.

So I've got to start from the very beginning. The day before we left for Florida. Just an ordinary day.

Chapter 2

That afternoon, my best friend Margie Crotty and I stopped at the candy store for chocolate cigarettes to practice smoking. Cigarettes were rationed during the war, like everything else, but now there were stacks of packs, Lucky Strikes and Old Golds and Camels. And Chesterfields, so smooth they soothed your throat. That was what the advertisements said.

Margie and I believed in magazines and movies more than church. We knew that if we practiced hard enough, one day we'd smoke a real cigarette with Revlon *matching lips and fingertips* while Frank Sinatra sang "All or Nothing at All" right at us.

It was 1947, and the war was over. Now there was music on every radio, and everybody wanted a new car. Nobody had a new car during the war — they weren't making them — and nobody took pictures, because there wasn't any film. One thing about a war? You never have new.

But now our fathers and brothers and cousins were home, and our Victory Gardens had been turned back into lawns, because now we could buy not only what we needed but what we wanted, vegetables and coffee and creamy butter. Cameras and cars, and brand-new washing machines, even. Appliances were the reason my stepfather was getting rich.

We were lucky enough to live in Queens, where you could put a nickel in a turnstile and ride the subway to Manhattan, the place where everybody in the world wanted to be. They left the lights burning in the skyscrapers all night long, because now they could.

Summer was ending, and we were just starting to imagine a chill in the air. School would start any minute — next week, in fact. Margie and I were spinning out summer as long as we could.

Margie held her candy cigarette high in the air, even though ladies don't smoke on the street. We couldn't imagine being wicked enough to smoke on the street, but it was something to shoot for, something that smacked of high heels and saying "damn" if you broke a nail. In the meantime, we were careful not to step on the cracks in the sidewalk. Step on a crack, break your mother's back. We'd been saying it since we were nine years old, and it was just like Holy Communion. We believed in it absolutely, no matter how screwball it sounded.

"So much more fun to do this when it's fall," Margie said. "When it's hot, it just melts."

"It's even better when it gets really cold, because we can blow out real smoke," I said.

"I'm going to start smoking when I'm sixteen," Margie announced. "I don't care what my father says."

"And wear lipstick," I added, even though I knew my mother's "no lipstick until you're eighteen" rule was as unbreakable as "no roller skates in the house."

We both pretended to take deep drags, like Joan Crawford in *Mildred Pierce.*

"Why is a bad guy called a heel?" I asked.

"Is that a riddle?"

"No, it's a question."

Margie regarded the end of her candy cigarette. She tapped it lightly, as if to dislodge the ash. "Because he's the lowest of the low?"

"Then why isn't he called a sole?"

"You're asking the wrong question, Evie."

Well, wasn't that so Margie. She always had to tell you what you *should* be doing or what you *should* have said.

"What's the right question, Margie?"

"Why do girls always fall for heels?" She giggled a little too loudly, and I knew it was because we were passing Jimmy Huggett's house. Jimmy was Margie's idea of a heel, because he had black hair as thick as motor oil and he called out "hey hey" to girls as they walked by. Margie always walked slower in front of the Huggett front gate.

I knew I was just being sour-grapey. Even if I wanted Jimmy to notice me, he'd rather catch a line drive right in the eye. Margie, however, had "developed" over the summer. "Talk to me when she's twenty — she's going to be fat," Mom said, but for now, Margie was fifteen with curves, and I wanted them. I was dying to wear the full-skirted dresses Margie did, with a thick wide belt, but Mom said I had to wait until I could fill out a sweater.

We were passing the church now, so we hid the cigarettes in our skirts, even though they were candy, just in case Father Owen came out. In my neighborhood, everybody knew you, and if they didn't know you, they knew your mother or your priest.

Margie crossed herself as we passed the statue of Mary, but I got distracted. Up ahead was my crush, Jeff McCafferty. Walking with Ruthie Kalman.

Ruthie could fill out a sweater.

"Margie," I said. "Look."

She grabbed my hand and squeezed it, and suddenly I was sorry I'd pointed them out.

"Oh, nausea! Maybe they just bumped into each other, and they're going the same way," Margie whispered, even though they were half a block away. I smelled chocolate and satisfaction on her breath. Now she could console me. I'd been noticing lately that Margie had grown a sense of authority along with her breasts. Who knows, maybe her mother had laid out womanly wisdom on her bed along with her new brassiere. Mrs. Crotty had six kids. She ran a snappy household. Systems for everything.

Ruthie Kalman had thick dark brown hair and dark eyes with eyelashes so long it was like they were glued on. She lived in an apartment, not a house, which made her exotic.

I had seen them talking before. Suddenly I realized how *often* I'd seen them talking.

"Jeepers, Evie, you shouldn't worry," Margie said. "After all, a McCafferty won't date a Kalman. She's Jewish." She whispered this last word, as if the statue of Mary would blow a raspberry if she heard it.

I knew Margie was right. That's the way our neighborhood worked. But Ruthie was so pretty that anything could happen. I knew from just looking at him that Jeff

8

was in love with her. I could tell by the back of his head, which I knew like clockwork. I'd stared at it all through geometry last year. If I could tell when he suddenly understood the isosceles triangle, I could get this.

It was almost worse that he couldn't have her. It was all Romeo and Juliet and balconies. Ruthie had European cousins who disappeared into camps during the war. She was so lucky — tragedy *and* curly hair.

"C'mon," Margie said, and she began to walk faster. I followed, because when somebody expects you to follow them, you have to go ahead and do it.

We were just behind Jeff and Ruthie, close enough that I could see the fraying on the collar of her white shirt, which she tried to cover with a polka-dotted scarf. Ruthie was always well pressed. She had the cleanest fingernails I'd ever seen, even after a whole day of school. I felt better seeing that flaw.

"Je-eff . . ." Margie sang out his name like a tune.

Jeff half-turned but didn't stop walking. "Hey, Margie. Hey, Evie."

"Aren't you supposed to be at the altar boy meeting? I just saw Father Owen going into the church."

Jeff stopped. "Aw, get out. There's no altar boy meeting."

"Wanna bet? Frank was just going." Frank was Margie's older brother. We'd just seen him taking off to

9

play baseball. I looked at Margie. Why was she telling such a whopper?

"Sorry, Ruthie," Margie said. "I guess your people don't know about altar boys."

Jeff looked down the block to the Virgin Mary, whose hands were outstretched, palms out, as if to say *What gives?*

Ruthie slipped her books out from underneath Jeff's arm.

"You'd better go, Jeff," she said. She didn't look at him. She looked at us.

He had a chance to say no. But he mumbled "See you" to all of us and headed back toward the church.

Ruthie turned and began to walk.

"Do you believe the nerve?" Margie whispered to me. "Did you see the way she looked at us? I'll show her."

"Let's just go home."

"Come on, Sister Mary Evelyn," Margie said. She called me that when she thought I was being a goody-goody.

Margie speeded up until she was right behind Ruthie. She stepped on the back of her loafer and gave her a flat tire, flattening the back of the worn leather so that Ruthie's foot came out of the shoe.

"Sorry!" Margie chirped out the word like she was in glee club, smug because she had the solo. Fat chance. I had a much better voice than she did. So did Ruthie. She stood next to me in glee club because we were both tall.

Ruthie reached back to fix her shoe but couldn't do it without stopping. She hopped for a few steps, trying to hook her fingers behind the heel. Then she gave up and walked on the back of her shoe. Her gait had a hitch to it now, but she only went faster, scuffing one foot along the pavement to keep her shoe on.

Margie tried to speed up to follow her, but I yanked on her shirt. Ruthie lurched along, faster and faster. She turned the corner and disappeared.

"We sure showed her," Margie said.

"Yeah," I said. "I guess we did."

Chapter 3

When I got home, I slumped down on the glider on the porch, hoping my stepfather, Joe, would be there. I wanted someone to tell me I was beautiful, even if he was lying. I wanted to forget that picture of Ruthie walking away, dragging her foot along so she wouldn't lose her shoe.

Of course, Margie had done a best friend's duty. She'd staked out my territory. Loyalty counted the most in my neighborhood. I should have felt lucky to have a best friend who would fight for me.

The door opened behind me, and Mom sat down on the stoop, her skirt billowing and then drifting down to her ankles. Unlike other moms, she wore her good clothes all the time and didn't care if she got them dirty.

My mother was beautiful. I always said that first, because it was the first thing everybody noticed.

I took after my father.

You couldn't stop looking at her. She was a knockout. The way she held a cigarette, the way she danced in the kitchen, the way she could make supper with a cocktail glass in one hand — that was movie star glamour. You could almost forget she was just a housewife from Queens.

"In the dumps?" she asked me.

"I want to wear lipstick," I said.

She took a cigarette pack out of her apron pocket, then her gold lighter. She tapped out the cigarette, then placed it between her lips and lit it. She took a fleck of tobacco off her bottom lip. She was wearing Revlon's Fatal Apple lipstick — *the most tempting color since Eve winked at Adam.*

"Don't be in such a hurry to grow up, baby," she said, blowing a plume of smoke out toward Mrs. Carmody, who was sweeping her porch and pretending not to spy in windows as the lights came on. "It's not all polka dots and moonbeams, you know."

"It's got to be better than this," I said.

"You think so?"

A breeze ruffled her blond hair. She stared out into the air and flicked an ash off her cigarette.

I leaned backward over the glider and looked at her upside down. Her face seemed to assemble into something foreign. Her blue eyes looked like triangles, and I could see straight up her nostrils. It was strange how a face was just eyes, nose, and a mouth. It was how they were arranged that counted. I was cheered to discover a position in which my mother was not quite so lovely.

Even though I didn't say a word, she knew. "You're too young for boys, anyway," she said.

"You got married when you were seventeen," I pointed out.

"Good Lord, Evie, you don't want to take after me. Anyway, I was a mature seventeen."

No kidding. I have one photograph of her and my father. She looked hubba-hubba even then, in a flowered dress, clutching the arm of my father, who was leaning back on his heels, like he wanted to fall backward into another life. Six months later, he did. He brought her a cup of coffee in bed, said he was going to California, and walked out. She was seventeen and already pregnant with me.

Now she looked at her watch, the one Joe had surprised her with for their anniversary last year, the one he'd bought in a fancy jewelry store on Fifth Avenue. ("You're crazy," she'd said. "We can't afford this." "Let me worry about it," he'd replied. "And I'm not worried.")

"Your father is late," she announced. "Again. Be

prepared for a roast like a rock. I can't wait to hear what Grandma Glad says."

My grandmother's name was Gladys, but Joe wanted us to call her Grandma Glad. Maybe it fit a vision of what he wanted her to be, the opposite of what she really was. She knew how to spread misery around.

Mom took a puff of her cigarette. "Maybe she'll break another tooth."

The living room window was open. "I'm not deaf yet!" Grandma Glad yelled.

Mom raised her eyebrows at me, and I had to slap a hand over my mouth to put the plug in my laughter.

So that's how we were: a mother and a daughter sitting on a porch, laughing as the tree shadows stretched toward the porch and lights came on in the houses. Sounds cozy. But it was just like buzz bombs — the V-2 rockets the Germans launched at London near the end of the war. You couldn't hear them, not even a whistle. Until your house blew up.

Chapter 4

After they got married and Joe knew he was going overseas, he insisted we move in with his mother. Suddenly we had a house with a porch and a yard. Grandma Glad made us pay rent, but it was her house, after all. It must have been hard to give up two good bedrooms for the duration. But I'm guessing it was harder to say no to Joe because he was a soldier. We all felt like we had to make sacrifices on the home front. It made us — the women — feel braver, and better, if we were suffering, too, somehow. Even if it was only arguing in the kitchen.

Mom got a better job at Lord and Taylor while I was in school. She was the best saleswoman in the tie department, her manager said. She came home at 5:45 on the dot. Grandma Glad had figured out how long it took to walk from the store to the subway, and how long it would take to wait, and how long the ride was, and how long the walk was from the subway to home. If Mom was late, she wanted to hear why.

You could say that Grandma Glad raised me from age nine to thirteen, but usually I spent whole afternoons at the Crottys'. Mostly I remember Gladys plopped in the gold armchair, listening to *Amanda of Honeymoon Hill* on the radio and watching the clock like a factory foreman ready to dock Mom's pay. I knew she considered minding me as her patriotic duty, right up there with hoeing our Victory Garden. Tomatoes and her son's stepdaughter — we both broke her back.

Grandma Glad was always saying things to Mom like, "My, what a bright dress, Beverly" or "Maybe you need to go up a size on that sweater." I could guess Mom's reaction by how hard she stubbed her cigarettes out in the ashtrays. If you came into the room and saw them ground into little stumps, you knew that Mom and Grandma Glad had just had a chat.

Mom smashed the boiled potatoes in the pot, twisting her wrist, her bracelet jingling. Joe had brought it back from the war, and it had real rubies in it. Everything was cheap over in Europe now, he said. You could pick up stuff for practically nothing. The poor folks over there were glad to sell it. You were doing them a favor.

She paused every once in a while, and I poured in a little milk from the bottle. We'd been making mashed potatoes together since I was four. It had been just the two of us back then, sleeping in the same bed in the little apartment over the candy store. Then Joe had walked in, with his hat on the back of his head and his eyes on Mom, and changed everything.

I stuck a spoon in the pot and took a bite. It was dark out now and steam had clouded the kitchen window. I heard Joe's car, and I ran to the window and made a circle with my fist to clear it. I saw him get out of the car, and for a minute I saw a stranger, his hat pulled over his eyes, his shoulders slumped in a way I didn't know.

That happened sometimes. He was away for so long, and even now, if he turned a certain way, or if I saw him on the street, it was like he was just another man in a suit. I let out a breath, and the window fogged up again.

I hurried out into the hallway, hoping Grandma Glad hadn't heard the car door. If she had, she'd be the first one at the door to greet him. But I saw the armchair pulled up next to the radio, and her wide back hunching forward to listen.

The door opened, and he walked in. I hadn't turned on the light, so he didn't see me at first. I saw his face, and he didn't know I was looking.

It was the war. You couldn't ask him about it. You

didn't want to remind him. What every wife and daughter could give was a happy home. That was our job.

That's what the magazines said. I clipped articles for Mom and left them on her chair. Recipes and new fashions, all the things a wife could do to make herself more attractive to her husband. Mom had quit her job at Lord and Taylor the day after he came back. "Either that or get fired," she'd said. She had to make way for the veterans who needed jobs. Now she learned recipes and made Sunday suppers, rubbed Jergen's lotion on her elbows, and had time to be a wife.

"Son of a bitch," he said.

I almost stepped back into the warm steam of the kitchen. This wasn't the Joe I knew. He was a muscular man who made walking look like dancing. He had a special greeting for everyone on the block. He made up nicknames that stuck. He could flip a cigarette butt into the gutter, hail a friend, and toss a chocolate bar to a kid from the neighborhood without breaking his stride. I'd seen him do it.

So I switched on the light to make the magazine picture. The daughter welcoming the dad home, both of them so happy in the picture you could practically smell the pot roast.

I held out my hands. He punched his hat back into shape and then held it by the brim. He closed one eye, like he was aiming, and then spun the hat down the hallway toward me. I snatched it out of the air.

"The Dodgers need you, kiddo," he said. I hugged him and felt his whiskers, smelled cigarettes and the special sweet scent that came off his skin.

As I hung up his hat, Mom came out of the kitchen.

"Aw, Bev," he said, apologetic even before she spoke. "How am I going to keep you in mink and diamonds if I don't work late?"

Mom turned around, her arms out. "You see a mink here?"

Joe winked at me. "Well, maybe if you give your husband a kiss, Santa will be good to you this year."

"It's still summer. You've got to do better than that."

He walked to her and slipped an arm around her waist to draw her against him. She bent back a bit to look at his face.

"You started without me again," she murmured.

"Just a quick one."

They didn't move. She was bent back in his arms, one hand on his chest. Suddenly I was just like the chair, or the hat rack — just a stick of furniture in the room. Back then they were everything I knew about glamour. Everything I knew about love.

Grandma Glad poked her head out into the hallway. "Someone called for you, Joe."

My mother's mouth turned down. It was funny, how the two of them competed, even for the telephone. It made Grandma Glad happy to be able to give Joe his messages, like she outranked Mom.

"It's the same man who called before," Grandma Glad said. She folded her arms over one of the dark blue dresses she always wore. Some of them had flowers and some of them had dots, but they all looked the same. "The one who asked about you, were you the Joe Spooner from the Forty-second."

"Oh, for crying out loud! Next time he calls, tell him I'm not home," Joe said. "Another ex-GI looking for a job. I'm home now — I want to eat dinner and relax."

This wasn't like Joe. Usually he was happy to talk on the phone. He'd bellow into the receiver while he crossed his ankles and leaned against the wall. He'd say, "Hello, Al," or "Bill, how do?" And then, "Terrible, how are you?"

Joe had what *Every Young Girl's Guide to Popularity* called "easy charm." I didn't have it. It didn't seem to be something you could learn from a book, either. When girls at school called out, "Evie, how do?" I wished I could yell back, "Terrible, how are you?"

Grandma Glad disappeared back into the living room.

"I wouldn't look so forward to dinner if I were you,"

Mom said. "The potatoes are glue and the roast is overdone."

She said it like a challenge. Joe only grinned. "Whatever you cook, I'll eat, Gorgeous."

In the kitchen, Mom shoved the roast onto a platter. Joe poured himself his drink, Canadian Club on the rocks, and mixed Mom a Manhattan. He sat at the kitchen table. We heard the phone ring, and he took a long sip. He bared his teeth, sucking in the liquor, and then began rolling up his shirtsleeves.

Grandma Glad appeared in the doorway. The kitchen light flashed on the lenses of her rimless glasses, and I couldn't see her eyes. Her hands were folded over her shelf of a bust, like she was already apologizing for interrupting, even though she never apologized for anything.

Mom looked annoyed. She liked Grandma Glad to stay in the living room before dinner so she and Joe could have a drink and a cigarette together. If Grandma Glad came in early, she let her know it, down to the second.

Mom said the house was too small now. I knew that she and Joe kept arguing about moving, and whether they had to take Grandma Glad. When they got tired of that, they argued about where to move. My mother wanted an apartment in the city, but Joe kept reminding her of the housing shortage. He wanted to move out to Long Island or New Jersey.

"We've got the American Dream, Bev," he said. "But there's more of it out there."

"Not in New Jersey," my mom replied.

Now Mom banged the spoon on the pot, flicking off a dollop of potato. "Dinner's not ready yet, Grandma Glad," she said.

"I can see that," Grandma Glad said. "It's the same man on the phone, Joe — he says he must speak to you. Or he'll drop by later, if you're busy now."

Joe's fingers curled around his whiskey glass. He stood up. "Christ, can't a man in his own house —"

"Joe!" Grandma Glad's hand flew to her mouth, as if she was the one who'd let the Lord's name escape her in vain and was trying to stuff it back in.

"Enough, Ma," Joe said, and pushed past her.

"Well, he's in a mood," Mom said.

"Probably he's hungry," Grandma Glad said, with a long glance at the kitchen stove. Then she clomped out in her red slippers.

"And it's my fault the dinner is late," Mom muttered, banging a pot lid on the stove.

She reached over to take a sip of the cocktail Joe had made her. "Did you set the table?"

"Yes, ma'am."

She nodded, still frowning, as if she was sorry I'd done it, because otherwise she could have yelled at me.

23

She scooped the mashed potatoes into the bowl, metal spoon against china, *snap, snap*. I heard the burp of the gravy as it was poured in. Then the ladle, clattering against the gravy boat.

It seemed like a good idea to disappear before she thought of a chore I hadn't done. I edged out of the kitchen into the hall. Grandma Glad was standing right outside the doorway, so intent on eavesdropping that she didn't see me. She always eavesdropped when you were on the phone, even if I was just talking to Margie about homework.

"Yeah," he was saying, "you wouldn't think so, would you? Got to be a hundred Spooners in the New York phone book, though. Sure, sure. Good luck, fella." He hung up.

"Joe —" Grandma said.

"Ma." He shook his head. She moved closer, because she never took a hint. They started talking in low voices. I beat it back to the kitchen.

Mom had the serving pieces all lined up on the table to take out to the dining room. I picked up the mashed potatoes and was heading out when Joe reappeared in the doorway. His face was red, as though he'd been the one bending over the stove. He tapped his empty cocktail glass against his leg as if he was keeping time to a jazzy rhythm in his head.

"So, does he want a job?" Mom asked.

"Doesn't matter, he got the wrong Spooner." Joe leaned against the doorway as Mom turned. He watched her as she brushed her hair off her forehead with the back of her hand.

"Look at your mother, Evie," Joe said. "A beauty like that shouldn't be stuck in Queens, right?"

Mom snorted as she took butter out of the icebox.

"A beauty like that should be lying around a pool, going out to restaurants, shopping all day. Not have her face in a hot oven. Right?"

"Right," I said.

Mom was trying to ignore us. "Don't be his stooge, Evie."

"So what would you say if we left tomorrow morning on a trip to Florida?"

"For crying out loud, Joe."

"I'm serious. Not just Florida — Palm Beach, the ritziest town in Florida. I got the car all gassed up, ready to go. So what would you say?"

"I'd say I have no clothes."

"Buy them there."

"I'd say you're crazy."

"Like a fox. I was thinking about it today. I've been working too hard. It's time for a vacation, since we didn't take one this summer."

"That's what I said back in July." Mom jerked her head toward the living room. "Is she going?"

Joe spread his hands. "Honey, I've got to at least ask her —"

She turned her back and began to swipe at a clean plate with a dish towel. "Then I'm not going. Have a good time with Gladys."

What about me? I wanted to ask. But I clammed up. I knew when to talk, when to make a joke to get them talking to each other again, and when to watch and keep my mouth shut.

Joe poured himself some whiskey and drained it. "Into the breach," he said, heading out to Grandma Glad.

Mom kept rubbing that plate. We could both hear the murmur from the living room, and I was dying to go listen, but I didn't.

When Joe came back in, he headed straight for his drink. He winked at me over the rim. "After dinner, we'll pack," he said. "Grandma Glad isn't coming. She doesn't want to miss Sunday Mass with Father Owen."

Mom leaned against the counter. I watched them look at each other. I expected Mom to be happy, give Joe a kiss. But she didn't.

"Palm Beach!" I said. "It sounds so fancy!"

He sat on the chair and patted his knee. "Come on, Bev. Let's blow this joint and have some fun, the way we

26

used to. Everybody needs some fun once in a while."

"You seem to get your share," she said.

Mom doesn't give in easy. She took her time folding the dish towel and placing it back on the counter. Then she walked over and sat on his knee.

"I've never been to Florida," I hinted.

I sat on his other knee and slung an arm around his neck. "C'mon, Joe. I've never even been south of Jersey." *Don't stick me here with Grandma Glad*, I prayed.

Joe laughed. "You don't have to give the soft-soap, Evie." He put his arms around us both. "I can't do without my two beautiful girls."

"What about school?" Mom asked. "Evie starts next week."

"Evie doesn't need school. She's smarter than her teachers."

"Can I get a white bathing suit?" I asked.

"Sure. You'll be a regular Rita Hayworth. Now," he said, giving us both a squeeze, "I'm starved. Get me a saw and I'll carve the roast."

I laughed, leaning back against his shoulder. It felt reckless and crazy, like we could do anything, jump in the car and drive hundreds of miles, just to chase summer.

It didn't feel like anyone was chasing us. Not at all.

Chapter 5

The trip took four days and three flat tires. Long days of driving on two-lane roads, passing trucks loaded with squawking chickens in Delaware, and cars with salesmen driving with their hats on outside of Washington, and trucks loaded with apples in Virginia. At first we sang and read magazines out loud and Mom passed back cheese sandwiches.

Maybe Joe's jokes became a little too jokey. Maybe we had the fizz, but only because Joe was shaking up the soda bottle so hard. Because pretty soon we weren't talking much, and we just wanted to get there already. Joe stopped trying to entertain us and started speeding, watching out for local cops.

The farther south we got, the warmer it grew. At first we loved the heat, cranking down the car windows and tossing our sweaters in the trunk. But then it was not just warm, it was hot.

At home, when it was hot, relief was a fan, a glass of

lemonade, and maybe a bus ride to Rockaway Beach. But there was no end to this. Just hot metal and hot road, until sweat stuck us to the seats and we just wanted to dive into any shade we could find. Except we couldn't; we had to keep on driving.

Joe's left arm was sunburned from where it hung out the window. He wet a handkerchief with water and put it on the back of his neck.

We started getting up at five A.M. to drive in the cool part of the day. We quit by three. Mom made Joe find a motel, or a guest house. Each place had stained chenille bedspreads, and rust stains around the drains, and toilets that Mom scrubbed first before she let me sit on them.

I cheered when we crossed the Florida state line. Dust billowed and blew in the window, and even the glimpse of the ocean was just a cheat, because when we stopped and pulled over to wade in the water, we were itchy with sand and salt when we dried off.

Mom unstuck her legs from the seat, one after the other, then lifted herself up and spread her skirt underneath.

"You said it would be warm," she said, fanning herself with her hat. "You didn't say it would be hellfire and damnation."

"What do we care? We'll be in the pool all week," Joe said.

"If we ever get there," Mom said. "Are we driving to South America? You in trouble with the law, Joe?"

"Shut up, Bev!" Joe snapped.

My mother jerked her head to look out her window. They didn't talk for another fifty miles.

Just before dark we drove into West Palm Beach, straight down a busy street with drugstores and a movie theater and people walking with ice-cream cones. I hung out the window like a dog, lapping it up.

"Now this is more like it," Mom said.

"Wait till you see the ritzy part," Joe said. He turned onto a small bridge and we drove over the water. "You see? Palm Beach isn't just a beach, it's an island. You don't have to mix with the suckers back there on the mainland. This place belongs to the rich."

Now it belonged to us. Tall palm trees marched down a row, taller than any palms I'd seen so far. Or maybe it just seemed that way because they were *rich* palm trees, the way I thought of Humphrey Bogart as handsome just because he was a movie star. I knew we were heading toward the ocean because I could smell it. And then there it was, still blue against the lavender sky.

The houses that lined the road were as big as hotels. They were painted in the colors of summer dresses, pink and yellow and cream.

"What gives? They're all boarded up," Mom said.

I noticed the closed shutters on the windows, like the houses had their eyes shut tight. There was nobody walking on the street. No cars driving by.

"Where is everyone?" Mom asked.

"They're all in their pools, counting their money," Joe said.

"There's a hotel!" I sang out.

Joe slowed down, but it was closed.

"Is this Palm Beach or a ghost town?" Mom asked.

I saw Joe's mouth twist and I was afraid he'd tell her to shut up again. "Look at all these flowers!" I said. "I bet there's lots more hotels. This is Palm Beach."

There were other hotels. Plenty of them. But they were all closed. Huge, grand hotels like palaces. Smaller hotels with courtyards with dry fountains.

"Let's go back to West Palm," Mom said.

"I said Palm Beach and it's going to be Palm Beach," Joe told us. "So the place closes down in the summer. Things will be opening up. It's fall."

"I thought you said you made a reservation, Joe," Mom said.

They both fell silent after that. I was the only one talking, pointing out houses and trees and the blooming bushes, explosions of pink and purple. Mom had her window cranked down all the way and tapped her finger

31

on the door. I could smell Joe's perspiration from the backseat and see the stain on his shirt.

Then, just when I was sure he'd have to give up, he turned down a side street and we saw it. A hotel with a light on. And it was pink. Pink as cotton candy.

"Le Mirage," I said, reading the sign.

"Well, it does feel like we crossed a burning desert," Mom said.

Joe drove down a circular driveway that ended under a porch. "Look at this fancy drive, just made for a Cadillac."

"Too bad we're driving a Ford," Mom said. But she said it in a funny way, and we all laughed again.

A skinny boy in a red jacket and black pants suddenly came running out to open our doors before we could. "Welcome to the Le Mirage Hotel," he said as Joe got out of the car and stretched his back. The boy held out his hand. "Your keys, sir. I'll get your bags."

Mom and I linked arms and caught our breath when we walked into the lobby. It was almost cool inside the tiled space. It looked like a castle, only smaller. There was carved wood everywhere, and whenever they could add gilt, there was gilt.

"It's like Radio City," Mom said, hugging my arm.

"There's a painting on the ceiling," I said, tilting my head back.

A tall man and woman strolled across the lobby toward the dining room. The man touched the small of the woman's back as she walked. She wore a pink dress with a deep neckline and a black sequined cardigan draped over her tanned shoulders, fastened with a brooch. Her black hair was long, past her shoulders, and straight. It was pinned to one side with a clip that looked like a spray of diamonds but were probably rhinestones. She wasn't beautiful — Mom had her beat by a mile — but she was the kind of woman who made heads turn.

"Now there's an attractive couple," Mom said in the voice she used when she approved of something, like Gregory Peck in *Duel in the Sun* or Butter Rum Life Savers. "I wonder where they're from."

"Jersey City by way of Kalamazoo," Joe said, which is a joke he makes if he means "nowhere and everywhere." But you could tell he was happy that a little shot of glamour had turned everything around.

We wanted the whole hotel to be as good as the lobby, and it almost was. We liked the white tablecloths and the clean towels, as many as we wanted. I had my first grapefruit, smothered in sugar. We learned that the bright flowers were *bougainvillea* and how to plan around a thunderstorm every day at four. We had never seen rain like that, pounding so hard it seemed to jump off the sidewalks straight back into the sky. We liked the breeze off the ocean at night, and the tiny green lizards, and the smell of night-blooming jasmine. We all got the giggles just hearing Joe say "I'll charge it to our suite."

It didn't take Mom long to realize that we were too dumb to know what everybody else knew — nobody came to Palm Beach in the fall. There were so few guests in the hotel that Mom and I were able to nickname them all, like Nice Fat Man and Mean Fat Man, Honeymoon Wife and Honeymoon Husband, Crabby Couple. We called the glamorous couple we'd seen when we checked in The Swanks.

The rest of the hotels didn't even open until December. All of the stores on Worth Avenue, Palm Beach's main drag, were closed. The Paramount Theatre was closed. We had landed in a ghost town.

The desk clerk told us about things to do — tennis lessons, boats we could rent — but we never got to them. We started to notice the worn upholstery on the sofas and the stains on the carpets. The hotel had been closed during the war, and nobody had bothered to fix it up.

Mom finally met the swanky couple by asking for a light. Their names were Tom and Arlene Grayson. She'd once worked for Hattie Carnegie, the dress designer. He owned a "small hotel" in New York. That did it for Mom.

The Swanks became The Graysons, and Mom and Joe started staying up late to play bridge with them.

I started eating dinner early in my room, sandwiches and potato chips. I'd eat in my damp bathing suit to stay cool, sitting on the carpet. Then I roamed around. I got to know how a hotel worked. I saw the closets that the maids disappeared into to fill carts top-heavy with towels and stinky with soaps. I saw the bored clerk at the desk sneaking looks at a girlie magazine. I saw the valets sitting on the white stone wall, smoking cigarettes. I peeked into the lounge with the stuffed sailfish where Mean Fat Man sat drinking alone every night. I walked the halls and played hopscotch with a penny for a potsy, hopping from rose to rose on the carpet. I didn't have to worry about being childish. There was nobody around to get embarrassed in front of.

It's crazy how you can go from not being bored to being bored out of your mind in about the time it takes to tie your shoes. I started to wonder about school and Margie and Jeff and when we'd be going home. I missed lying on my bed, listening to Sinatra on the record player. I was tired of being hot.

And then one night everything changed.

Chapter 6

I heard the laughter first.

I crept to the window and looked out, still chewing on my chicken sandwich. The usually empty drive was filled with girls getting out of their daddy's cars, squealing and running to catch up with other girls who were posing on the steps while boys in white jackets stood close by, looking at them but not talking, not yet. Girls, peering into compacts, lying to each other about how pretty the other one looked. Girls in petticoats and stockings, hair brushed one hundred strokes, perfume from the bottle they got for Christmas. Girls laughing at nothing. Girls going to a dance.

They wore corsages and were dressed in foamy dresses with skirts that fanned all the way down to their ankles. During the war, skirts were shorter because we had to save material for Our Men in Uniform, but now that the war was over everything was bigger. Cars, buildings, skirts.

The perfume! I could almost smell it from the window. Jungle Gardenia and Evening in Paris. I hummed with all the wanting I had inside. I wanted to be those girls. I wanted to be blond like my mother. I wanted to have a dress with a full skirt.

I looked at them and I wondered: What would it be like to come as a stranger to a dance like that? At home, I would be one of the wallflowers, one of the ones a teacher would muscle a boy to ask to dance. Here, I could be anybody. Here, I didn't have to be me.

I opened my closet door.

Gloom. What I needed was tulle and net and petticoats and shoes dyed to match my dress. I had cotton dresses and white anklets and saddle shoes.

What I needed, of course, was a fairy godmother. But I wasn't Cinderella.

I didn't even have to touch my hair to know what a mess it was. I hadn't washed it after swimming in the ocean that day. It was thick and wiry with salt, not glossy and groomed the way it should have been, like the bouncing pageboys out the window.

I wandered into Mom and Joe's room through the connecting door. Mom had gotten dressed in a hurry and had left her compact behind, open on the mirrored vanity. A dress was flung on the bed, something she'd rejected. High-heeled sandals were kicked off underneath it. A towel stained with powder was draped over a chair; bobby pins were flung like jacks on the dresser.

I opened the closet. Shoes kicked off and left on the floor all crazy, nylons in a little silky ball. A woman's closet. Not like mine, which smelled of salt water and perspiration.

Her perfume rose from the dresses and the beach-wear. I passed my hand along the dresses. Lots of them were new; Joe had followed through on his promise to buy her clothes. I pretended to hesitate, but there was only one dress I really wanted.

It was spring-green silk with violet flowers scattered on it, and if that combination sounded ugly, it wasn't. The funny thing was, I didn't think it looked so swell on Mom. The pale green color didn't suit her. I liked the deep V of the bodice and the pleated sash. It would fit me, I knew it. But I needed one of her bras, and tissues to stuff inside. Plenty of tissues.

I flung the dress on the bed alongside the other one. I felt greedy as I pulled out a lace brassiere that stood up at attention in the drawer. I didn't look in the mirror while I slipped my arms through the straps and stuffed it until there was no gap between the material and my skin. Then I slipped into the crinoline petticoat, all stiff and crackling with purpose.

I was just adjusting the tissue in the bra when the door opened and my mother and Mrs. Grayson walked in. I had my hand right in the cup.

Mrs. Grayson's eyebrows arched over her dark eyes like blackbird wings. My mother had a cigarette in her hand with a long ash. I watched as it dropped to the carpet.

We all froze, like we'd been flung into our poses like a game of statues.

Then they laughed.

Mrs. Grayson put a fist to her mouth, but her laugh came out like a little yelp. They leaned against each other and giggled like girls.

I looked in the mirror. My hair was frizzy. My arms were skinny and I was too tall. I looked like a dog on its hind legs. I felt tears spurt into my eyes, and my humiliation was complete.

"No, no," Arlene Grayson said. "We're not laughing at you, petal. We were just surprised, that's all." She clicked over to me on her high heels. "You look pretty. You just need a few . . . touches."

I smelled their cocktails and their hair spray and their confidence in their own allure. "She's in such a hurry," Mom murmured to Mrs. Grayson.

"Weren't you?" Mrs. Grayson asked. "I was. We need to fix her hair, Bev." She was all cool and soft, like iced sweet butter. She tucked my hair behind my ears. "We should wet it down."

My mother looked at the green dress I'd flung on the bed. "I know one thing. She doesn't need a girdle like I do for that dress."

"Look at that waist," Mrs. Grayson said. She placed her hands around my waist. "Those were the days. Come on, Bev, let's fix her up."

Mom hesitated, but I knew she wouldn't refuse Mrs. Grayson. They pulled me forward, digging for lipsticks and combs. I felt part of a conspiracy, a conspiracy I'd always watched from the sidelines, girls pulling their friends into powder rooms, or pinning broken bra straps.

They dragged me to the sink and mercilessly ran a wet comb through my tangles, laughing at the faces I made. They put setting lotion on it and pushed it one way, then the other. Mom fussed over me with lipstick and powder while I felt my hair being tugged into a French twist. My back was to the mirror so I couldn't see what she was doing, only the line between her eyebrows as she concentrated.

"Don't look yet," Mrs. Grayson warned me. The amusement in her voice was gone now. She was taking the job seriously. Hope made bubbles in my chest. If anyone could make me pretty, I thought, it was Mrs. Grayson. Mom had always put the kibosh on my attempts to be pretty. She said I had plenty of time. Mrs. Grayson seemed to understand that I didn't.

Mom cradled the dress in her arms like a newborn and carefully pulled it over my hair. She did the hooks in back. Then she pulled down the skirt in a professional way. Mrs. Grayson brought over a pair of high-heeled white sandals. I slipped into them and wobbled.

"Keep your head up," Mrs. Grayson ordered. "Don't look at your feet. Straighten your spine!"

I straightened my back and lifted my chin.

"Good," they said together.

"Now look," my mother instructed.

I looked in the mirror. I expected to see a version of my mom. Somehow I'd hoped that the dress would look better on me than on her. It didn't.

"Smile," Mrs. Grayson said, and I smiled. "There. You're beautiful."

She said it seriously. Not like Joe did — and I realized at that moment that when Joe said I was beautiful, he always lumped me in with Mom, as though I was the giveaway and she was the real prize. *Sure you're beautiful, kid — look where you came from!*

In the mirror, I exchanged a glance with Mrs. Grayson. I was surprised to see sadness there.

She leaned over to speak in my ear. "This is your time, Evelyn. Grab it."

Just one dance. Just one. That's all I wanted.

I know now how you can take one step and you can't stop yourself from taking another. I know now what it means to want. I know it can get you to a place where there's no way out. I know now that there's no such thing as *just one*. But I didn't know it then.

"Come on," Mrs. Grayson said. "Before you turn into a pumpkin."

They spun me around and pushed me out the door, wobbling like a top winding down. Now I had no choice. I went.

Chapter 7

uckily the band was playing, and mostly everyone was dancing. I walked straight to the punch bowl and poured myself something red in a crystal cup. I did it slowly, hoping that some boy would come over and offer to pour for me. No one did.

I stood with my back to the gold brocade curtains and watched, sipping the sweet warm punch, afraid to spill on Mom's dress.

I figured out pretty quick that everyone in the ballroom knew each other. I overheard conversations and realized that they were all seniors in the local high school across the water, in West Palm Beach. This was the first dance of the year.

If I were pretty, a doll, a dish, maybe some of the boys would have gotten up the nerve to come and introduce themselves. But I saw their glances slide off me, like ugly was Vaseline, and I was coated with it.

I felt like I was disappearing. I clutched the punch glass, empty now. I couldn't seem to move to put it back on the table. If I moved a muscle, someone would notice me. The best I could do now was hope to stay invisible and then sneak out.

Then the worst thing happened. A boy noticed me.

He was the most unattractive boy in the room, a dog-face, a Poindexter, the one who hadn't asked any girl to dance, because he knew that no girl wanted him to. But I was a stranger, so he figured, why not?

I realized that there was something worse than not being asked to dance. It was being asked to dance by the wrong boy.

He pushed himself off the wall as the band swung into "In the Mood" and the swirl of dresses took over the dance floor. I was trapped, caught between the dancers and the punch bowl.

"You don't recognize me, do you?" he said. "Which makes us even. Because it took me until now to recognize you. Swell dress." He waited another second, then said, "I'm a bellhop here. And I park the cars."

"Did you sneak in, too?"

"I go to the high school," he said. "You're the sneaker. Maybe I should call the manager."

I couldn't tell if he was serious. But a Florida kid wasn't going to get away with that with me. "Go ahead,"

I said. "Let's see what happens. Maybe it will liven up this lousy party."

He grinned at me. "I'm Wally."

"Evie."

"Yeah, I know. We know all the names of the guests. Not hard, since there's hardly any. You should see this place in December."

"So I hear."

"So what do you say? Do you want to dance?"

He was so far away from my dream of what this night could be. I saw three pimples on his chin, and how the comb marks were still in his hair. One of the prettier girls looked over and whispered to the boy she was dancing with. She giggled.

"No, thank you," I said. "I . . . don't want to dance. I have to go, anyway. See you around!"

I had to get out, and fast. I turned and put down my punch glass and then pushed at the French doors behind me. I felt the breeze on my face. The air was like water I could dive into and swim away in.

The pool looked so impossibly blue with the lights on — a blue I had never seen before in my life, not in the sky or the ocean or a dress. It was the cleanest blue I could imagine. I felt calmer just looking at it, and at the way the lights under the water made the shadows of the palms waver.

I felt a chair at the back of my knees, and I sat, petticoat crackling. I wanted to rip the whole dress off and tear my hair out of the hundreds of bobby pins Mrs. Grayson had stuck in my head (my scalp, I'm sure, was dotted with red pricks from each individual pin). Suddenly I was furious at them, at Mom and Mrs. Grayson, for dressing me up, knowing how stupid I looked, and launching me at that party like a battleship.

I took off one of the high-heeled sandals, the white sandals my mother prized, and threw it into the pool.

That's when I noticed him. He was on the other side of the pool, dressed in a white shirt and khaki pants. He had lowered the chair until it was flat, and he was lying back on it, face to the night sky, smoking a cigarette. He raised himself on his elbows and looked into the pool like he owned it.

"Well?" he said.

I didn't say anything. Was he going to report me to the manager, a man who smelled like Vitalis and only smiled at the rich guests?

"Aren't you going to let the other shoe drop?"

I took off the other one and threw it in.

"My kind of woman," he said.

Woman. From across the pool, in this dress, did I

look like a woman? If I could just manage to beat it out of here, victory would be mine.

But then there were the shoes. I could maybe think of a reason they were soaked. (What? A waiter spilling a pitcher of ice water? A toilet overflow?) But I couldn't come up with a reason for them to be lost.

He stood up and started toward me. It took him a while to get to me because he had to walk around all the chairs and the deep end of the pool. I had plenty of chances to run, but I didn't. There was something that made me stay. I was afraid to be rude, I guess.

I'd always been such a good girl.

He sat on the end of the chaise next to me. He didn't look at me, but looked at the pool. "I'm more used to taking orders than giving them, but you do know, don't you, that it's a crime to be sad under a full moon."

But you do know, don't you ... You could hear the commas in his sentences. Nobody in Queens talked like that.

My feet dangled off the side of the chair. It was the only part of me he could see. I was embarrassed by my sunburned toes.

"I assume that you're a refugee from the dance inside."

"I escaped the enemy, captain," I said.

I could see the side of his face, and his smile. "Ah," he said. "At long last, a promotion."

He turned and I saw him under the moon. My breath stopped. He was not just handsome, he was movie star handsome. Dark blond hair, a straight nose. *A hunk of heaven*, Margie would say.

"I was only a private," he said. "Disappointed?"

I shook my head, because how could I be disappointed in anything about him?

"But I do know," he continued, "how to salvage an evening for a girl in a party dress."

He stood up, bowed. Held out his hand. "May I have this dance?"

"Here?"

He frowned. "Oh, wait." He sat back down, and I felt disappointment thud inside me, even though I wasn't about to dance with him — that would be crazy. I didn't even know his name. He bent over, and I saw that he was untying his shoes. He dropped them and then stripped off his socks. His feet gleamed white in the moonlight. It seemed awfully forward to stare at them, so I looked away.

"I don't want to break your toes," he said. "I'm not a very good dancer."

He stood there with his hand out. I was too embarrassed to take it.

"And they danced by the light of the moon, the moon, the moon." I blurted this out, and my cheeks flared with heat. What a stupid thing to have said, to have quoted a nonsense poem! "The Owl and the Pussycat." Now he'd really think I was a child.

But his grin was slow and easy. "So come on, pussycat," he said.

This time I took his hand.

It wasn't as awkward as I thought it would be. Not after a minute. My dress crackled as we moved slowly around the deep end of the pool. He hummed. I recognized the tune.

For all we know, we may never meet again.

I wished Mom and Mrs. Grayson could see me now.

But then I didn't. This was better if no one saw. Better if it was my secret.

Every so often, our ankles brushed against each other, our toes. It felt like the most real thing that had ever happened to me. I was part of the hot, dark night. The night was all breath and air. I was all skin.

I had to remember every detail. His ankles. His fingers. The golden stubble on his cheek.

And then I forgot everything except the dance. I was able to dance for the first time in my life, really dance, and understand why it worked, one body against another body.

This may only be a dream. . . .

Chapter 8

The next morning, I sat at the small round table on the patio, so I could see the pool where we met. I forced myself not to look up every time someone came through the door.

He had walked me to my door last night. He had bent over my hand but hadn't kissed it. He'd said, solemnly, "Thank you for the dance." He had handed me my wet shoes, the shoes he had fished out of the pool with a net he'd found by the lifeguard chair. He'd never asked my name. Instead, he'd called me pussycat.

"Good night, pussycat," he'd said.

The usual people came to breakfast, the same guests I saw every day. Crabby Couple always ordered poached eggs, and I had to look away because, really, the sight of that runny yolk and the way they dipped their toast and didn't talk to each other made me feel so sad. Honeymoon

Husband always ate alone. Nice Fat Man was on his way to Miami, he kept saying, but he still hadn't left. If you got up early for breakfast in this hotel, it could be the loneliest place in the world.

I looked at myself in my spoon. I felt like the girl I saw, upside down and fun-house looking, all stretched out of shape and foolish, just from holding so much want inside.

Then the door opened and he walked in.

He stood next to my table and smiled down at me. He was wearing light-colored trousers and a white shirt with the cuffs rolled up.

Forearms. Who knew they could be so beautiful? I looked at the worn leather of his watch strap. Everything else faded away but the blond hair on his arm against that strap.

"I was hoping you'd be here," he said. "I forgot to ask your name."

If only, if only, if only, I had a pair of sunglasses. Then I could have tilted my head back and looked at him, and he wouldn't have been able to see my eyes. I could have pretended to be mysterious — something I couldn't do with my naked, freckled face.

"Evelyn," I told him. "Evie."

"Good morning, Evie. How are your eggs?"

"Cold."

"Well, at least something's cold here. May I join you?"

He was sliding into a chair even as I was nodding. He picked up a napkin and shook it out. "Peter Coleridge. Glad to meet you." He signaled the waiter. "Bring another plate of eggs for my companion —"

"No, really —"

"Toast and coffee for me, as hot as you've got, and orange juice, cold as you can make it," he said. Once again, I admired how he talked, not ordering the waiter, exactly, but there was an undertone that made the waiter say "Yes, *sir*" very snappily and hurry off.

Top drawer. That's what my mother would call it.

"I drove in last night," he said. "I couldn't sleep, it was too hot. So I went outside. I was feeling melancholy. Then I danced with a beautiful girl, and I felt better. What's your story?"

He looked at me expectantly, as if I was the kind of girl who had a story.

What would Barbara Stanwyck say? She always played a tough-talking dame. *"It's no fairy tale, mister,"* she'd shoot back, and Dana Andrews or Ray Milland would say *"That's okay, baby, 'cause I'm no prince."*

"I don't have a story," I said. "I'm still waiting for one."

"Well," he said, "that can be a very interesting place

52

to be." His long fingers reached out for his coffee cup, which the waiter had just filled. "I'm thinking of going down to Delray for lunch today," he said.

Delray. The offhand way he said it made it sound like the nightclub El Morocco in Manhattan. I was sure that it had to be the most stylish place in Florida.

"Where is that?" I asked.

"Just a bit south of here. It's a town where people actually live, as opposed to here. People only live here in the winter. So Delray is a bit more lively."

"Oh."

"My point being, would you like to join me?"

I had two thoughts, and they didn't match. The first was how green his eyes were. That was a good thought. The second was, I must have heard wrong.

Of course it was a no-go. My parents would never let me go off with a strange man — because Peter (the name! perfect!) was a man, not a boy — and if he knew I was only fifteen he would take back the invitation, pronto. But didn't I *look* fifteen, sitting there in my blue skirt and brown sandals?

I was saved from answering when the waiter put a plate of eggs in front of me and brought him toast and juice. The juice glass sat in a little metal dish surrounded by ice. The steam clouded up from my eggs. I took a bite and burned my mouth.

He took a sip of coffee. He looked at me over the rim. "Any girl who throws her shoes into a pool is someone I'd like to get to know."

I was sure that if he knew me better, I'd bore him. Girls like me bored young men. I'd been known to bore twelve-year-old Tommy Heckleman, from down the block.

"I can't," I said. "I'm fifteen."

He took his spoon and scooped out marmalade onto his toast. "Don't fifteen-year-olds eat lunch?"

"I'd have to ask my parents."

"Then ask them."

"They'll say no."

"Then don't ask them. It's an old army trick."

A page turned in my mind. It had never occurred to me before that I could do something without permission. "May I" was a way of life for a girl like me.

"Think fast!" Tommy Heckleman would yell as he'd fire a baseball at my head.

But I didn't have to make a decision, because right at that moment my mother walked out onto the patio. I didn't have time to prepare; she saw us immediately and headed over. She had her dark glasses on, and her blond hair was still a little tangled from sleep, as if she'd just barely passed a brush over it. Just my luck — she was never up this early.

Peter stood. He said good morning.

She said good morning and arched an eyebrow at me.

"This is Peter Coleridge," I said. "Peter, this is my mom."

This was wrong, somehow, and I knew it. This was the way I introduced friends to my mom in Queens. Surely there was a more polite way to do it now, a way I'd never learned.

She sank into the empty chair at our table.

"Pleased to meet you," Peter said. Then he explained, "I met Evie last night," as he sat down.

Mom twisted around, looking for the waiter. "I came down for coffee," she said. Her voice sounded thick, as if she wasn't quite awake.

He was all business then, raising a hand for the waiter, who instantly appeared. "Another cup," he said, "and make it hot." Then he turned back to Mom and said, "I come here in the winter. This is the first time I've been in the fall. They weren't open during the war."

"Nothing was open during the war," Mom replied. The waiter brought her coffee and she dunked three cubes of sugar in it. Sugar rationing had just ended that summer and we still weren't used to having as much as we wanted. She stirred it, her spoon clanking, and then took a long sip. She closed her eyes briefly, then regarded Peter again. "You look too young to have served."

"Should I be pleased or insulted?"

"Take your pick."

"I'm twenty-three. I was just telling Evie that there's more to see down here than Palm Beach."

"I've been to West Palm." Mom shrugged her tanned shoulders. "We bought a pineapple."

"There's a place down in Delray that will cure what ails you."

"What makes you think you know what ails me?"

"I can only guess. I was just telling Evie about Delray, about taking a run down there. Why don't you join us?"

The conversation swiveled back to me. Mom regarded me for a moment, as if she'd just noticed I was there. "Where?" she asked.

"A place called the Tap Room. Ever been there?"

"The world is full of places I haven't been," Mom said.

"Gets a good crowd. Locals, the airmen from the base. Though I warn you — if you do come, you just might start a rumor that Lana Turner came in."

"Lana Turner . . ." Mom rolled her eyes, but you could tell she was sucking that compliment down with her coffee. Lana Turner was every man's dream, sultry and blond. It was Lana filling out a sweater at a drugstore that got her a Hollywood contract.

"Come on down and give them a thrill."

She reached over to his pack of cigarettes on the table and extracted one slowly. She tapped it on the table while she gave him a long look. She placed it between her lips and he leaned over to light it, cupping the flame against a nonexistent breeze.

In that gesture, in the way they leaned together, and how she took a drag and leaned back — it was like a dance I didn't know. Right at that moment, I decided to learn.

Mom blew out the smoke and crossed her legs. She swung one foot in her platform sandal.

"You can ask your husband, too," Peter said.

"Ask him yourself," she replied, and lifted her hand to wave.

And there he was, coming through the door. He was wearing a wrinkled shirt and a grumpy expression.

"I woke up and you were gone," Joe said to her. He was so crabby he didn't seem to care that Peter was sitting there. He didn't even give him a glance.

"I had a headache. Joe, this is . . ." She started to turn, but Peter suddenly stood up, the metal chair scraping against concrete.

"For crying out loud, it's Joe Spooner!" Peter said. "How are you, Sarge?"

Peter put out his hand, and Joe just looked at it. He gave him a hard stare, like he was trying to put together who he was. Peter withdrew his hand and put both hands in his pockets.

"Peter Coleridge," Peter said. "I was only a private, but surely you remember me. I was just sitting here with your wife and daughter — isn't this such a coincidence? I drove down from Long Island. What are the odds of this?"

Joe squinted at him in a sour way. "You'd be surprised how many GIs from my old outfit I run into. They come out of the woodwork."

"Joe doesn't talk about the war," Mom said.

"What's the point?" Peter said, nodding. "The thing we remember is the buddies we made. That's it."

"Some of the buddies I'd prefer to forget," Joe said.

"Say, I'm with you there. Some of them, sure. But you make a buddy in the army, you have one for life. I remember how you talked about your wife all the time." Peter turned back to Mom. "Guys, they exaggerate. They describe Betty Grable and you see their snapshot and she looks like Olive Oyl." Mom laughed, but Joe yanked out a chair so hard it squealed against the concrete. I'd never seen him in such a bad mood. "But Joe here, he didn't exaggerate, not a bit. I can see why he made it home in one piece. And it's clear he's a successful man."

"He has three appliance stores," I said.

"We all talked about what to do after the war," Peter said. "Joe always had the big ideas."

"What about you, Coleridge?" Joe asked. "What are you doing down here?"

He shrugged. "My old man has some business interests down here. I was going to take care of that, maybe go down to Miami. But I'll be here for a while."

"Peter was just telling us about a place in Delray that's a good time," Mom said. "He wants to take a run down there."

"You're invited, too, of course," Peter said.

I crossed my fingers underneath my skirt like a kid. Please. Please, please, please. Say yes. Fathers got the last word. If he said no, we didn't go.

"Come on, Sarge," Peter said. "We've been through some times together. You know I'm on the up and up. Just like I know you are. Right?"

Joe's thumb flicked against the room key in his hand. "Why don't you girls run on upstairs?" he suggested. "I'll have a cup of coffee with Pete here."

I took the fact that Joe called him Pete, not Peter, as a good sign. I didn't hear then how Joe smacked his lips against the *P* and made it sound like an insult. I only heard the familiarity.

I followed Mom to the door of the hotel. My old blue

skirt swished flirtatiously against my legs as I copied the sway of her walk. We walked out together like two Lana Turners, leaving the men at the table watching us go. We could feel their gazes. We didn't even have to turn around to know it.

This could be the worst thing, even worse than everything that came after: Even now, if I could go back to that moment — I wouldn't change a thing.

Chapter 9

My life was always screwy compared to other kids' because my mother worked. She had to, from the time she was fourteen and her parents died after a subway train derailed at Times Square. They were on their way to the movies. She was taken in by her uncle Bill; there was nobody else. She worked in his Sweet Shop 'N Luncheonette every day after school, and that's where she met my father. She got married at seventeen, and after my father took off, Uncle Bill would slip her an extra dollar or two on rent day. Then he died, and Aunt Vivian never gave us an extra penny. Mom said we should be grateful the witch let her keep the job.

I always wanted a father. Any kind. A strict one, a funny one, one who bought me pink dresses, one who wished I was a boy. One who traveled, one who never got up out of his Morris chair. Doctor, lawyer, Indian chief. I wanted shaving cream in the sink and whistling on the stairs. I wanted pants hung by their cuffs from a dresser drawer. I wanted change jingling in a pocket and the sound of ice cracking in a cocktail glass at five thirty. I wanted to hear my mother laugh behind a closed door.

If I could choose a father, I would have chosen someone exactly like Joe. I fell for him, same as her. I was a pushover. I dressed up when he was coming. I laughed at his jokes and made sure we had beer in the fridge, even if we had to do without milk to buy it.

Joe and Mom had a date every Wednesday and Saturday for a year. Plenty of Sunday afternoons he'd take us for an outing, Rockaway Beach or even the city, just to get a soda at a drugstore. We waited forever, both of us, for him to propose. Christmas was coming, and Mom wanted a ring, or at least a promise. Joe couldn't afford a ring. He'd lost his job at the hardware store during the hard times and did a little of this, a little of that, to stay flush. A couple of nights pumping gas, three afternoons a week delivering seltzer and soda.

Mom was beginning to lose hope, and on Sunday mornings, after her date with Joe, she was starting to slam the coffeepot around something awful instead of humming to herself.

Then came Pearl Harbor, and we listened to the president's speech like everybody else, staring at the radio like we'd miss a word if we looked anywhere else. I was only nine, so I knew that something terrible had happened but at least it wasn't my fault. Later that night we heard feet pounding up the stairs, and it was Joe. He said we were in for it now, and everybody was saying Germany would be next. He said he was going to enlist, and asked her to marry him on the spot. My memory of his proposal is all mixed up with the voices on the radio talking about death and fire and lost ships in a place I'd never heard of, and Mom sobbing into Joe's shoulder.

Everybody seemed to die or disappear on us, so you could see how Mom and I lived through the war years with our fingers crossed, waiting for Joe to return. I stood over her on Saturday nights when she wrote him, telling her things to put in that I'd thought up all week, things to make him miss home so he'd fight stronger. I knew he wouldn't die. Not with us to come home to.

Four years went by. He had furloughs, when he'd show up handsome in his uniform and we got to parade him around, each of us holding on to an arm. Then he went back, and we got to worry and study the newspapers and his V-mail, just like everybody else. He felt even farther away when we got that mail, as if his personality had been squashed into the letters that were photographed and shrunk by Uncle Sam.

Joe didn't come home until a year after the war ended.

"Just a bit of mopping up to do," he wrote to us. He was stationed in Salzburg, Austria. I knew right where Salzburg was, because we'd stuck a big map on the wall in the kitchen. Everybody's geography got better during the war. I knew where Normandy was, and the Philippines, and Anzio, Italy. I could stick a pin in them right now without hardly looking. Pin the tail on the battle, Mom used to say. And pray Joe's not in it.

Those last months were the worst. It seemed like every day someone else's father or husband or son came home, and there was a party in someone's living room or backyard. When Margie's father came home, she walked around in a glow for weeks. I almost hated her. *Your father was only a private*, I wanted to say. *Phooey.*

We didn't talk about it, but I knew what my mom was feeling, because it was just what I was feeling. It was like Joe had been a dream.

And then, suddenly, one April morning, Joe returned, blowing in the front door with his arms full of flowers. I remember the splash of cold spring air on my cheeks, how he kept the door open and even Grandma Glad didn't close it. All the neighbors came over to say hello and stayed until one in the morning. General Eisenhower himself couldn't have gotten me to bed that night. I was wearing a present Joe had brought back, a bracelet that I kept twisting around on my wrist. Real gold, he said.

I never took the bracelet off, even in the bathtub. I never once thought about who'd owned it before. I was too busy pushing up the sleeves of my sweaters so everybody could see it.

Within two months of coming home, Joe had opened his first appliance store in Queens. "How do you like that?" he said. "Everybody wants to loan me money now." Then he opened another in Brooklyn, and he was planning to open two more. Everyone wanted to buy a brand-new Bendix washer from the Spoon.

When they got married down at City Hall, a photographer was there from *Life*, the magazine that was on every coffee table in America. He was looking for servicemen who were tying the knot. So Joe goes right up and tells him the story, how he'd stolen Beverly Plunkett, the prettiest girl in Queens, how he was called "the Spoon" and she was called "the Dish."

But here's the thing: Mom never had a nickname. Joe made it up. He conjured up the headline he wanted right out of the air, like Mandrake the Magician. He sold it the way he sold appliances.

The picture was on the mantel, in a silver frame. In it they're jumping off the third step of City Hall down to the sidewalk, arm in arm. Her blond waves are bouncing, her mouth dark with lipstick. It is in the very middle of winter, snow on the sidewalks, husbands and brothers and fathers heading off to war. But look at Beverly Spooner. Nothing ahead but blue skies. You can see it in her gleaming teeth, in the gardenia on the lapel of her camel hair coat, in the way one of her gloved hands is bunched into a fist, ready to punch Herr Hitler's lights out if he gets in the way of her happiness.

Over their heads, the headline hollers:

AND THE DISH RAN AWAY
WITH JOE SPOON

I was there that day, at City Hall. Mom asked if I could be in the picture, too. I saw the photographer's gaze move over me, a plain-faced nine-year-old in my plaid coat, my legs all goose-bumpy from the cold. He took the picture, but even then I knew it wouldn't be the one they'd pick. I wasn't a part of that glamour, that glow. In the article they didn't even mention me. It was like Mom got married for the first time.

We'd stopped at a bar before we went. I waited outside with the corsage in a box. I felt very important. Grandma Glad had refused to come. I would be their only guest. Good-bye, Evie Plunkett, I kept saying to myself. Evie Spooner. Evie Spooner. The new name tasted like strawberry jam. I would get that, and a dad, too.

66

Chapter 10

In the end the Graysons came, too, and we all drove down to Delray Beach in their brand-new Cadillac. We sat on a terrace in the shade, where we could feel an ocean breeze. Everyone ordered hamburgers. I sipped on my lemonade, pretending it was a cocktail.

Mom and Peter and the Graysons kept the conversation going. All the things grown-ups talk about smashed together: the weather, would the Commies get the bomb, did you hear Fiorello LaGuardia was in a coma, Peter's home in Oyster Bay, Long Island. You could tell he didn't want to brag about it, because he changed the subject to the Graysons. Peter had heard of the hotel Mr. Grayson owned, the Metropole, and he said it was one of the best in New York. You could see this pleased Mr. Grayson. He was a thin man in horn-rimmed glasses who looked more like a professor than a hotel guy; he didn't look like an easy man to win over, but Peter did it so smoothly.

As the adults talked, I couldn't seem to punch a hole in the conversation. I couldn't capture his attention, not like I had the night before. I felt young and stupid again, with my glass of lemonade and my brown sandals.

Joe chomped on his hamburger moodily. I'd never seen him like this, grumpy and looking old in the bright sun. When he turned to signal the waiter for another beer I could see his scalp through his hair.

"Everybody wants to just jump in a car and go these days," Peter said. "Especially ex-GIs. I enlisted the day after graduation. I drove down to New York from New Haven."

"Ah, a Yale man," Mr. Grayson said.

"Then I had three years of being told what to do and where to go. Enough already. Right, Joe?"

Joe didn't answer. He had a big bite of hamburger in his mouth.

"How about you, Tom?" Peter asked.

"4-F," Mr. Grayson said. "Bum ticker."

No one said anything for a minute. Back home it was the biggest shame, 4-F. Unfit for service.

"What I felt over there was, the fellows that couldn't fight, they held the country together. They gave us something to come back to," Peter said. "My brother John was 4-F, same as you. He did more for the war than I did. Worked as an engineer in a defense plant. All I did was slog through a couple of acres of mud. John was the real hero." He said it seriously, giving Mr. Grayson a look of respect. Mr. Grayson's shoulders relaxed, and Mrs. Grayson looked grateful.

Mom took a sip from her glass. "Mmm, I can't get enough of this orange juice," she said. "Have you ever had anything like it, Arlene?"

"Never," Mrs. Grayson said. "They keep the best oranges for themselves down here, I guess."

"Rats live in orange trees," Joe said. It was the first thing he'd said in a while.

"Don't be morbid, Joe," Mom said.

"Who's being morbid?" Joe asked. "They need their vitamins, just like we do."

Mrs. Grayson laughed.

Mom hadn't touched her hamburger. I pushed mine aside. The meat seemed heavy and ancient, something that would soon be stinking in this heat.

Tom Grayson's forehead was shiny with sweat. "I found out why our hotel is open in the off-season," he said. "It's for sale."

"You thinking of buying it, Tom?" Mrs. Grayson said, smiling.

"You think that's so crazy?"

"Yeah," she said. "I do."

"Maybe not so crazy," Peter said. "Now we've got the

gas to get anywhere we want. Lots of folks will be traveling."

"Exactly," Mr. Grayson said. He sat up straighter. "And wait until all the buildings are air-cooled. That will bring the tourists."

"I'm thinking of adding those units to my business, selling to restaurants and hotels," Joe said. "There's a market out there."

"Here's where you should be selling them," Mr. Grayson said. He cleared his throat, as though he was just waking up. "I'm telling you, this place is due for a boom."

"Joe here is a smart businessman," Peter said. "He knows when to grab the big chance. Right, Joe?"

Joe didn't answer Peter. He nodded at Mr. Grayson, as though they were the real businessmen in the group because they were older than Peter.

Peter didn't care. He turned to Mom. "How about you, Beverly? Do you think Florida is going to boom?"

"People like to start fresh," she said, looking at him from under the brim of her big straw hat. "You won't go broke betting on that."

He laughed softly. "Paradise seems like a good place to do it."

"Maybe paradise is overrated."

"Lady, you are one tough customer."

Mom's lips curved. "Me? I'm just a softy."

"We should all go fishing one day," Joe said. "Rent a boat and get out on the water."

"I don't like fishing," Peter said.

"You feel sorry for the little fishes?" Mom asked.

"Yeah," Peter said. "I feel sorry for anything that gets hooked."

"I love boating," Mrs. Grayson chimed in. "Tom and I used to go in the south of France, before the war. Those were the days, really. We didn't think anything could change." She stubbed out her cigarette. "What we need is some coffee."

Mr. Grayson twisted around, looking for the waiter.

I felt panicked. Was the lunch over already? I hadn't said more than two words.

"Who's game for a walk?" Peter asked.

I stood up quickly, almost knocking my chair backward. "I'll go."

"Don't worry, Sarge," Peter said to Joe. "I'll take good care of her."

We walked out of the courtyard and down the street toward the beach, toward the pavilion there.

Peter leaned over and spoke in my ear. "We finally ditched the chaperones. Come on."

He took my hand as we ran across Atlantic Avenue. He linked his fingers through mine and swung our arms.

We walked to the pavilion and he dropped my hand. We looked out at the ocean instead of at each other. All I wanted to do was hold his hand again.

The breeze picked up, and we faced right into it.

"You're a watcher, aren't you?" Peter said. "I can tell. You watch and listen. But you know what I'm betting? The thing you can't see so clear is yourself."

I was startled. Here I was, trying to come up with something to say about the weather, and he said something real. "What do you mean?" I asked.

"You don't walk like a girl who knows how pretty she is, for one thing. That's a crying shame."

"Once I heard Grandma Glad tell someone that I was as plain as a bowl of Yankee bean soup," I said.

I expected him to laugh, but he didn't. "Your problem is that your mom's such a looker. You get all balled up. You can't even see what's in front of you in the mirror. So you've got to listen to an older brother type like me. You're pretty."

An older brother type. That stung.

"If you were an older brother, you'd call me Rubber Lips," I said. "That's what Frank Crotty back home calls me."

"That's because he likes you."

"Frank? He only thinks about the Dodgers."

"Pussycat, you've got a lot to learn about boys."

I pretended I was Barbara Stanwyck and tossed my hair. "Yeah? Who's going to teach me?"

He smiled. "Now that's a tempting assignment."

The weather had changed. I hadn't noticed how low and dark the clouds were. The ocean was now a flat dull gray, thick and molten-looking.

The first fat drops began to fall, but he didn't move.

"A tempting assignment," he repeated, "but I'm going to pass. I should stay away from you, pussycat."

I couldn't say anything. Of course he would stay away. What man wouldn't?

"At least, I'm going to try," he added.

The sky opened up, and the rain hit us hard. We stood there, looking at each other. I started to shiver because I knew something was happening. Something adult and mysterious.

He grabbed my hand and his grip was warm and wet and tight as we ran through the raindrops back to the others.

Chapter 11

I spent most of the next day strolling around the lobby trying to walk like I knew I was pretty. I saw the guests come and go: Mrs. Grayson off on a bicycle with a big bag in the front basket, Mr. Grayson and Joe driving off together, Honeymoon Wife heading for the pool. I waited and watched and waited some more. It didn't seem possible that I wouldn't see him again. Not after the way he'd looked at me. Not after the way he'd said *At least I'm going to try.*

His car wasn't in the parking lot, and I felt desperate and crazy. Finally as dinner approached I thought of something. I went up to the desk and waited for the manager to notice me. In my hand I had a piece of hotel stationery (getting damper by the second) that said:

Thank you for lunch. I had a lovely time with you.
Hope to see you soon! Evelyn Spooner

At the last moment I almost walked away because I realized the exclamation point made me sound like sap.

"I'd like to leave a message," I said when the manager looked up at last. "For Mr. Coleridge."

Mr. Forney had a tiny mustache and thin dry lips. He gave me a look like I was a bedbug who'd crawled out of the honeymoon suite. "Mr. Coleridge has checked out," he informed me.

I turned away. My head spun, but I walked across the lobby anyway, not knowing where I was going.

The boy who'd asked me to dance, Wally, came up behind me and said, "He left yesterday. No forwarding address or anything."

I hadn't even thought to ask about a forwarding address. "It doesn't matter," I said. I shrugged as I slipped the note into my pocket.

"Just thought I'd tell you," he said.

I hated when it got dark, because it meant that I would have to go to sleep without seeing him. Mom and Joe were still talking in the lobby with the Graysons, lingering over a nightcap. So I left the hotel and walked. I kept thinking if I walked far enough, went down the right street, I'd run into him. But the streets were empty, like they always were.

I came back to the hotel late, but Mom and Joe didn't seem to care about curfews here. "What could happen?" Joe had asked, silencing Mom's "but . . ."

Under the trees I saw two people together as one shadow.

"No," the woman was saying, her voice angry and broken with tears. "I won't do it. You're going too far now. If you do it, you do it alone."

The door opened and one of the maids came out, carrying a garbage bag to the cans in back. The shaft of light illuminated Tom and Arlene Grayson.

Mrs. Grayson turned toward me, startled. Her face was wet, her mouth pulled out of shape. Then she yanked him away, farther into the darkness.

I was the only one at the pool early the next morning. I slid into the water slowly, letting my body fall until I hit the bottom and slowly rose again. I swam back and forth, back and forth. When I took a breath at one end, I saw Wally the bellhop watching me and trying to look like he wasn't watching me. Once he knew he'd been caught, he walked over.

The sun was behind his head and I couldn't see his face. "So, New York, why'd you come to the dance if you didn't want to dance?" he asked.

I flipped over on my back and kicked to keep

myself up. "Maybe I didn't think you could keep up with me."

He squatted down so he could see me. "Maybe I could."

"Maybe I'll never find out."

"Well, that's the last dance until December, so you're probably right. Your loss, I guess."

"I'm crying in my hanky." I flipped over and dived.

When I surfaced Wally was gone and I noticed Mrs. Grayson. She sat under an umbrella and was writing on a pad. She had a stack of postcards by her elbow. When I got out of the pool, she waved me over. I grabbed a towel and walked over.

She tapped the stack of postcards with the end of her pen. "Looks like we're the only early birds," she said. I couldn't see her eyes behind her dark glasses. "'Wish you were here' — doesn't everybody write that? They don't mean it, though, do they? I mean, what's the point of coming here if you don't want to get away?"

"Did you want to get away?" I asked.

A sudden gust of wind sent her papers flying. I took off after them, scooping up postcards as I ran. I put my bare foot down on a piece of hotel stationery. I didn't read it. Not exactly. But the words popped up.

It could all explode in our faces
It would be wisest to delay wiring it as long as you can

77

Then I saw her black sandal, and I quickly scooped up the page and handed it to her.

In one smooth movement she tucked it into her bag. She cocked her head and looked at me. "Do you know that Bev dresses you like a kid? I think I saw you in a pinafore the other day. Really! How old are you?"

"Sixteen in October. October thirty-first."

Her smile flickered for an instant. "Well, boo. It's birthday time. Let's go shopping."

I hesitated. I didn't want to leave. What if I missed seeing Peter?

"Darling, I have a tip," Arlene said. "Never, ever wait for a man. If I have to look at that blue skirt again, I'm going to scream. There's a shop in West Palm that's not bad. My treat, and don't bother to say no. We'll see what we can drum up in this hick town." Then she winked at me, as if I were a grown-up.

We both ran upstairs to change. Mrs. Grayson rapped sharply at my door. Mom opened it, still in her robe. I could hear the shower running and Joe blowing his nose.

"I'm taking your daughter on a spree," Mrs. Grayson announced. "No arguments, my treat."

Mom did not look pleased. "Arlene, I can't let you do that. Besides, she has plenty of clothes."

Mrs. Grayson put her hands on her hips. "Not from where I'm standing. This girl needs some glamour."

Mom smoothed my hair. "She's too young for glamour."

"I said no arguments. Now shoo." Mrs. Grayson flapped her hands at Mom. "Go have a nice long morning with your husband."

Mom held up her hands, as if Mrs. Grayson was about to arrest her. "Don't shoot, I give in."

Mrs. Grayson drove down Royal Poinciana, one hand on the wheel while the radio played Tex Williams singing "Smoke, Smoke, Smoke That Cigarette." I sneaked looks at her, trying to pinpoint her glamour. How did a woman do it, get you to think she was beautiful when she wasn't? She had a flat face and a wide mouth and small nut-brown eyes. It didn't add up to much if you saw her, say, with wet hair in the pool. But if you watched the way she moved through a room or bent over to pick up a drink, you couldn't stop watching.

Today she didn't wear a hat, just a scarf to tie her thick dark hair off her forehead. A puckered top was pushed down off her tanned shoulders, and a full striped skirt swooped all the way to her ankles. A wide silver bracelet with a turquoise stone slid up and down her arm every time she raised her hand to push her hair back or stab the cigarette lighter.

It was hard to remember her now the way I'd seen

her that night, with her face blurry with tears. It was like I'd dreamed it.

"Is Mr. Grayson really going to buy the hotel?" I asked.

She let out a noise — *ppffff* — as she made a left turn with the heel of her hand. "He just has a case of tropical fever, that's all."

Just then I saw a convertible ahead of us. It turned down one of the small side streets, toward the center of the island. My heart thumped, and I couldn't see for a minute. It was Peter's car. He was still here! If only he'd seen me, riding with Mrs. Grayson. Maybe we would have waved, maybe he would have followed us, maybe . . .

"The Breakers was a hospital during the war," Mrs. Grayson said. "There was a USO café on that corner. So they tell me. The war gave us so much, in a funny way, didn't it? It gave even the small-minded among us something to do. Now they have the Commie spies to focus on, I guess."

I'd never heard anyone talk about the war that way. Maybe it was because Mr. Grayson hadn't served.

"Did you lose anyone in the war?" I asked. It was a question you didn't ordinarily ask people, even if it usually ended up coming out anyway.

"Yes," Mrs. Grayson said. We were on Clematis Street in West Palm now, and she pulled into a space. She reached for her straw purse, and that was the end of the conversation. Usually people would give you names and battles, like "We lost my uncle Jimmy on Guadalcanal," or, "My brother John died on Omaha Beach." And you'd know everything, because you knew every battle in every country, every tiny island in the South Pacific, so you'd know the year and even the month.

But Arlene Grayson had only said yes.

Clematis Street was busy with people walking, shopping, dipping into the coolness of the shops. Mrs. Grayson jumped out, closing the door with her hip like she was doing the rumba. I saw a man literally stop in his tracks to watch her.

I followed her into a shop. She flipped through the racks, the hangers rattling with her speed. She politely ignored the comments of the saleslady — "This is a popular item" and "This peppermint stripe keeps you cool on hot days." I flipped through a few dresses and hesitated over a pink rayon nipped with a peplum and a long pleated skirt.

"No pink," Mrs. Grayson said, putting it firmly back on the rack.

My arms full of dresses, I stepped into the small dressing room. It was hot as blazes in there, and I was afraid of sweating on the dresses. I could feel Mrs. Grayson waiting, and I didn't know how long I had before her impatience would push us out the door. I tried on the first dress, seersucker with bare arms and a cinched in waist. I was surprised at how well it fit.

"Well? Let me see," she called, and before I could reply she moved the curtain back. She eyed me and twirled her index finger, indicating that I should turn around.

"Good. Try the print."

I tried on a rayon print with short sleeves and red buttons, but she shook her head this time. "Now the other one," she said.

I put on a full swinging skirt and a gingham off-the-shoulder blouse, similar to hers.

She nodded. "We'll take that, and the seersucker, and a pair of those white slacks. You can wear the blouse you have on with them. Take that bow off it, though. Borrow one of Beverly's scarves and use it as a belt. Show off that waist, dearie — one day it will be gone, I promise you. Now here. You need something for special occasions." She thrust another dress toward me, a pale blue evening dress, with a sweetheart neckline, bare shoulders, full skirt.

"We call that color moonlight," the saleslady said. "It's the prettiest dress in the store."

"Can we have a pair of high heels to try on with it, please?" Mrs. Grayson asked. Somewhere in her tone she told the lady to stuff her advice.

I slipped into the dress. Mrs. Grayson came in and smiled at me. "You're going to have to lose this," she said, and in one swift move she unhooked my bra and tossed it in the corner. I felt my face get hot. But her fingers were cool and practiced as she zipped me up and slid eyes into hooks. The dress pulled me in and up.

I put on the high-heeled sandals, shoes I could never, ever imagine wearing to school or church. The dress fit like a dream, tiny waist and a sweep of silk down to my ankles — a blue so pale and shimmering it was almost white.

"I can't let you buy me this," I said. "It's too much."

Mrs. Grayson looked at me in the mirror. "On every shopping trip, there is one indulgence. This is it." She slowly unfastened the back again. "The thing is, Evie, it will give me more pleasure to buy you these things than you know."

"Mrs. Grayson, I don't know how to thank you —"

"Have some fun," she said. "That's how. And stop wearing your hair like that." She reached over and took out the clips that kept it off my forehead. "Wear it loose. Part it on the side, and use pincurl clips at night." She smiled. "It's a good age to have your first romance. Just a little one. So you can go home and tell your best girl-friend about it."

She went to the counter to pay, and I scrambled back into my clothes, embarrassed that she'd seen what I thought I'd hidden. I wanted to tell her that I wasn't thinking of what I could impress Margie with. Not anymore. That would be something a teenager would do. I was already older, and I knew it.

He was underneath every word and every thought now. All I could think about was when I would see him again. It was the first time I knew what that kind of hunger, terrible and magnificent, was like. It was so much more than the words I heard in movies.

We pushed back out into the flattening heat of Clematis Street. Mrs. Grayson tossed the packages into the backseat of the car.

There was something about her I could trust. She talked straight to me, almost like I was a pal and not someone's daughter. The packages piled in the backseat made the car feel cozy enough for secrets. I had to tell someone who would understand. So I found myself blurting out my fear.

"I don't know when I'll see him again," I confessed, feeling the pain of each word.

"You'll see him in the hotel."

"No, he's gone."

"Petal, he'll be back tomorrow. He works there."

It took me slow seconds to realize who she meant.

"Cute kid," she said.

She thought I had a crush on Wally. The pipsqueak. That to her was a great match. Evie and Wally, sitting in a palm tree, K-I-S-S-I-N-G.

84

It was hard to be mad at her after she'd bought me all those clothes, but I managed it. We got in the car and I slammed the door.

"I'm not like other girls, you know," I said. "I've been taking care of myself since I was little. I'm not a kid. Mom worked since I was little. I made my own sandwiches for school since first grade. I put myself to bed plenty of times. Made the supper when she was tired. I did all that, and more, too."

I thought she'd understand, but she didn't. I could tell. She wasn't seeing me anymore. Now I recognized that other woman, the one I'd seen angry and turning her face away. All that pizzazz, and underneath it was a whole lot of sad.

"Okay, Evie," she said. "You're not a kid. Got it." She turned on the engine. "Just don't grow up too fast, that's all."

The mood had changed. Why had she invited me today? She'd asked me right after I'd read part of her letter. Was this shopping trip some kind of bribe? So that I wouldn't tell anyone what I'd read? So I wouldn't tell what I'd overheard?

It could all explode in our faces
I won't do it
If you do it, you do it alone

85

Chapter 12

The next day I sat with a schoolbook in my lap, under the shade of a tree that fractured the sunlight into points of fire. Numbers swam in front of my eyes. School seemed so far away. I was thinking of Peter, but I was also thinking of Arlene Grayson's suddenly cold eyes.

A hand reached over my shoulder and closed the book.

A flash of wrist, white cuff.

He whistled softly and raised me up, then stepped back to look at me in my new seersucker dress. I'd pulled in the belt as tightly as I could and my hair was loose and down to my shoulders.

"Well," Peter said. "Va va va voom. Look at you."

"You checked out." I blurted it out, then blushed, because it showed him that I'd been asking about him.

He sat on the wide arm of my chair. The sun hit his green eyes and turned the hair near the undone button of his shirt gold. "A friend has a house here — friend of the family. My father happened to tell him I was here at a hotel, and hoo boy, they were insulted. Peter can't stay in a hotel, et cetera. So I'm at their house. It was closed for the season, but I'm camping out." He took the book out of my hands and closed it. "It's too hot to read. Let's go to the movies. There's an air-cooled theater in West Palm."

My heart jumped around like a fish. I wished I could just leap up and go with him, without another word.

He knew why I hesitated, and he made a slight motion with his head toward the beach. "Your parents are down there. I'll walk with you."

We walked to where Joe and Mom sat under a tiki hut. I could see Joe talking while Mom looked out to sea. Peter waited while I slipped off my sandals.

"I hope he says yes," I said.

"Make sure and tell him I'll take good care of you," Peter said, shading his eyes to look down the beach at them.

I skip-hopped over the burning sand. I stopped in the back of the tiki hut, pausing a minute as my feet hit the cooler sand that was in the shadow of the grass roof.

"You've just got to have the big picture, got to grab the biggest slice of pie," Joe said as I hopped to the next cool piece of sand. He looked up at me, scowling, but I thought he was just squinting in the sun. I couldn't imagine that there would be a time that Joe wouldn't be happy to see me. His beach shirt was open, and perspiration snaked down his bare chest. Mom had just been in the water; her suit was wet, and drops sparkled on her legs. Her hair was pinned up on top of her head.

"Can I go to the movies with Peter?" I asked.

Joe blew out a breath and looked at the water. Mom drew a pattern in the sand with a shell.

"It's air-cooled, and I'm so hot," I said. "And he said . . . he said he'd take good care of me." Somehow it came out sounding wrong, but I didn't know why.

Joe twisted to look back up at the sidewalk where Peter waited. He stared for a long minute before he turned around again. "I don't like this, Bev," he said.

Mom shrugged. "She's almost sixteen."

"Which," Joe said, "is actually my point."

"So? It's just a matinee, Joe. Don't be such a stiff." Mom tossed her towel in her straw bag. "Tell you what — I'll chaperone. I've had enough sun anyway." She stood and wrapped the matching skirt around her tropical-patterned suit. She shaded her face with her hand and looked down at him. "I've had enough of this hot air," she said.

She didn't wait for Joe's good-bye. She hurried me along the sand, as if it was burning her feet, toward Peter. I was the only one to look back. I could see the back of the chair, and Joe's head, looking out to sea. His arm hung down next to the chair. His hand was curled into a fist.

The coolness of the theater made us shiver. Mom had changed into a white sleeveless blouse and a white skirt, and she glowed inside the darkness. Peter led us down to the middle section, close to the front. We were lucky. We came in during the newsreel.

The movie was *Dark Passage*, with Bogart and Lauren Bacall. Bogie's face was bandaged up, and I lost the plot about twenty minutes in. I just soaked up the darkness and Peter's arm next to mine. I could pretend that Mom was just a stranger on my other side.

But then the stranger nudged me. She put a whole dollar in my hand. "I'm starved," she whispered. "Get us something, will you?"

"I'll go," Peter whispered, and someone said "Shhhh!"

"No, Evie knows what I like."

I slipped out, bending down so I wouldn't get in anybody's way. I hurried to the counter. I didn't really know what Mom would want — she never really ate candy except in a big box on Valentine's Day. But I didn't want to waste any time out here so I asked for Sno-caps and a Hershey bar and popcorn. Then I put the change in my pocket and went back on a run.

I stood in the back of the theater for a minute, waiting for my eyes to adjust. Peter had moved over into my seat. Mom's blond head was close to his as she whispered something. The rest of the theater was dark except for those two blond heads, those white, white shirts gleaming in the darkness.

What I thought then was I needed to do that, think of a remark to tell Peter so I could lean with my lips close to his ear.

I slid into the seat next to Peter and passed the candy to Mom and the popcorn to him.

Peter held the popcorn in his lap. Mom and I dipped our hands in and out, occasionally bumping fingers, watching the plot tangle and untangle as the bad guys got shot.

It was mid-afternoon when we came out, the time of day when the heat bounced up from the sidewalk and slammed you in the face, and you felt like you could lick moisture out of the air.

"How about a soda at Walgreens?" Peter asked.

"A soda at the drugstore," Mom said. "That sounds keen!" She said it with a too-chirpy voice, and Peter grinned, even though I guess she was teasing him about being young, and not that nicely, either. He was a good sport not to get mad, and I wanted to kick Mom for being mean to him.

We sat at the soda fountain and ordered Cokes. The ice was crushed, and the soda was cold and delicious. There was a local high school crowd there, and I saw Wally again. He looked different now, in loose pants and a short-sleeve shirt, his hair unruly. Instead of looking younger, he looked older, my age. In his evening clothes and his bellhop uniform he'd looked like he'd been wearing his father's clothes. I was glad that he could see me now. I tossed my hair as I smiled up at Peter, just so Wally would know I was on a date.

He raised a hand to wave at me, and I gave him a little wave back.

"Friend of yours?" Mom asked.

"He works at the hotel," I explained.

"Why don't you go talk to him?"

"I don't want to."

Peter gave me the tiniest push at the base of my spine. "Come on. Give the fella a thrill."

I could feel that one tiny spot burning as I walked

over to Wally and said hello. "We've been to the movies," I said.

"Yeah, that's the way to keep cool. I saw that picture, too." Wally slurped up some soda and looked at his shoes. He didn't even know enough to ask me to sit down. "So, New York, have you ever been to the Empire State Building?"

"Sure," I said.

"How about Radio City?"

"You bet. You can get free tickets to the radio shows." I wondered if Wally was going to lead me through a list of New York tourist attractions. He was trying to make conversation, and he was a bore. Behind me I heard Peter laugh at something Mom had said. Was he being a good sport again? I was dying to get back so I could protect him from her.

"I went to Washington, D.C., once, before the war," Wally told me. "My dad is going to take me to Tampa."

"That sounds nice," I said politely.

"We go out on the boat every Saturday. It's not a big boat, but it's fun. There's plenty of stuff to see, neat places to go. Have you ever seen a cypress swamp?"

True, I was in a whole new state. But could it be that a boy was getting up the nerve to ask me to tour a *swamp*?

"You want a cherry Coke? I'll get Herb to mix you one."

"I'd better get back to my date," I told him.

"Your date?" He looked surprised as he looked over my shoulder at Peter and Mom. "Well, okay. See you around." No boy had ever asked to buy me a soda before. A month ago, it would have felt nice, even though it was only Wally the bellhop. Now it didn't mean anything, because all I could think of while I was talking to him was how quickly I could get back to Peter.

Mom was looking in her compact and Peter was tossing coins on the counter when I finally rid myself of Wally. It was the end of my date, and I'd hardly said more than ten words to Peter. On the drive back to the hotel I wondered how I could see him again. Ahead stretched an evening of cards and dinner and staring out the window at the moon. It seemed impossible that I could get through it without him.

He drove up to the hotel and parked. When he came around to open the door for us, he leaned in before we got out.

"Thank you for the company, ladies. Let's do it again."

Mom got out of the car and I followed, embarrassing myself by sticking to the seat as I tried to wiggle over. I tried to swing my legs out gracefully, the way Mom had.

Mom put out her hand, and he shook it.

"Thanks for the movie," she said. "And the keen soda."

"Anytime."

"Well," Mom said, slipping her hand out of Peter's, "I think I'll go for a walk down Worth Avenue and see if I can find a store that's open."

"I'll come," I said.

She shook her head. "Homework time."

I couldn't believe she'd brought up homework in front of Peter. I couldn't believe my parents had made me bring books to Florida in the first place. Furious, I watched as she walked off, her chiffon scarf trailing from her hand.

"You're a peach, Evie Spooner," Peter said.

And then he waited, just like in the movies, to watch me walk up the stairs into the hotel. When I turned around he was still looking. Behind him, my mother continued down the middle of the empty street, her scarf fluttering like some exotic tropical bird.

Chapter 13

All afternoon after the movie I lay on my bed and dreamed in a haze of heat. I built a future with Peter using geography and hope. He lived in Oyster Bay — a huge distance from Queens, and not just in miles. Out there they had lawns and big white houses and not a luncheonette in sight. But he had a car.

It was cocktail time and Mom wasn't back yet. I went to the connecting door and peeked in. Joe had changed his shirt and combed back his hair. As he waited, he smoked a cigarette and tapped his knee with his fingers in a constant Gene Krupa drum solo. He didn't seem in the mood for company.

Joe's impatience kept rolling through the open door. I could hear the drumming, hear him stub out another cigarette. Finally I heard him pick up the phone and call the front desk. He asked for Mom, then grunted, which meant she wasn't back yet.

"In another minute I'm calling out the marines, Evie!" he shouted cheerfully at me.

The tone in his voice gave me the nerve to ask the question I was dying to have him answer. We were stuck together waiting for Mom, so it seemed like the perfect opportunity.

I hovered in the doorway between our rooms. "What was Peter like during the war?" I asked, trying to make it sound like I was just making conversation.

Joe looked at me strangely. "Why are you asking?"

"No reason. I just never met a buddy of yours from the war."

"He wasn't a buddy. He just thinks he was. I didn't really know him. That's all I can tell you."

That wasn't much to go on. I wanted to ask another question, but I heard the click of her heels through the louvered door.

She walked in, her hair loose now and around her shoulders, carrying the ugliest vase I've ever seen. It was bright yellow and green, in the shape of a pineapple.

"What in the name of Sam Hill is that?" Joe asked.

Mom put it on the dresser. "A present for Grandma Glad." She smoothed her hair in the mirror.

"Bev, for crying out loud, it's past six. Where have you been?"

"I got my hair done. You never notice. And I did a little shopping." Mom came over and bent down to kiss me. I smelled Life Savers on her breath — and, behind that, something sweet. "Arlene told me about some of her favorite places."

Joe gave a doubtful look at the vase. "She should get out more."

Mom went into the bathroom to change. "Well, you're being an awful sourpuss."

"I wanted to talk to you. I have big news. Evie, this news is for you, too." Joe gave a dramatic pause as Mom came out of the bathroom in her slip. She tossed her white skirt and blouse on the floor of the closet.

Joe continued, "I had a very interesting afternoon with Tom. We're talking about going into business together."

"Oh." Mom crossed to the vanity. "Business."

"Tom is thinking of buying this hotel and he wants me in on the deal." Joe rolled out the words like a red carpet. He waited for Mom's reaction.

"What do you know about hotels?" Mom asked. "This is practically the first one you've ever stayed in."

"Tom knows. And I know business. We talked it all out today. We don't think we have much competition. Plus we've got a pretty good idea of what a swanky little hotel down here is like. We're thinking maybe a dress

91

shop in the lobby — that would be right up your alley, Bev. Let's keep it on the Q.T., though. Tom hasn't even told Arlene yet. And you don't want to get the word out there until you're set. You don't want the competition to find out and grab your deal."

"Yeah, the hordes are gathering." Mom began to powder her face. "And where's the money going to come from?"

"That's the beauty of it. I don't have to put up a cent right away, see. Tom can swing the price, he says. And then, down the road, I can buy my half out, bit by bit. After the stores sell and I get the money out of them, I pay off the debt load."

"How do you know the stores will sell?"

"They're a great investment!"

"You said you were overextended —"

Overextended. I realized that I'd heard that word before, back home, in boring conversations I wasn't supposed to be listening to.

"The new store in Brooklyn is in a dead location — how was I to know? The guy was a cheat who sold me that lease. What is this with the roadblocks?"

"I'm just trying to dope it out, Joe. What's the catch?"

"No catch. Look, I'm sick of selling appliances."

"Already? You said it was your ticket to being a millionaire."

"There's more than one road. This place is busting to develop. I'm sick of Queens — I've lived there all my life. Look at all the servicemen here, getting a taste of sunshine and orange juice. You think they want to head back home after this? Come on, sweetheart. Can't you see us here?"

"Big plans," Mom said. She was looking in the mirror, but she wasn't looking at herself, she was looking at the reflection of the window, out into the still strong sun of a tropical evening. It was like she already was bored with it, bored with this whole bright change that Joe was giving her.

She married a guy who delivered soda and pumped gas for a living and now he owned three stores. We'd been scroungers, too, all our lives, saving up for new shoes, sewing ruffles on the hems of my dresses when they got too short to wear. Now here we were sitting in a suite in Palm Beach. All because of Joe. So why wasn't she trusting his smarts?

Florida. Could Joe be serious? I tried on the idea. It meant leaving Margie and my school. I was surprised to find that it wouldn't break my heart. Margie would cry crocodile tears, send me two letters about how much she missed me, and then I'd never hear from her again.

I didn't know how I knew that, but I suddenly knew it was true.

People like to start fresh, Mom had told Peter. Everybody wants that sometime. Even when you're my age. Maybe *especially* if you're my age.

Peter's father had business interests in Miami, he'd said. And he seemed at loose ends. What if Peter moved here, too?

For one long moment, it all seemed possible. Now I was looking at Mom with as much concentration as Joe was.

Mom stood up and went to the closet. She picked out her white dress, the one with the full skirt embroidered in black and red thread with flowers. She held it out. "Here, Evie. This will look sweet on you."

"Really?"

I held the dress in my arms and hurried into my room to put it on. I could hear Joe through the door. I stayed close. I didn't want to miss a word.

"A little faith might be nice from my own wife. Maybe you just have a problem catching up. The war is over, I did my bit, and now there's money to be made. I'm not going back to what I was."

I pulled the dress over my head. I zipped it up myself the way I'd seen Mom do, squirming to get it up from the bottom, then the top. It fit like a dream. I loved the scooped neckline. It was a day dress, not an evening dress, but still.

"Nobody's saying that. I just don't know what Grayson gets out of the deal, that's all."

I could see Mom's point. Mr. Grayson and Joe were vacation pals, but what did he really know about Joe, and what did we really know about him?

It could all explode in our faces

I slipped into my new sandals. I walked out, hoping to get a reaction, but Joe was at the window, his back to us. Mom met my eyes in the mirror and smiled, then shrugged. That was the thing about Joe: If you crossed him, he got sulky. Mom always said that he needed one hundred and ten percent support.

Mom put down the brush in her hand. She looked at herself in the mirror, and I saw that it cost her something to stand up. But she did. She went over to Joe and put her hand on his shoulder.

"What do I know," she said. "I'm just a worrier. You know that. I'm sure it's going to be swell. Let's go down to dinner and celebrate."

"I'm not in the mood now."

"Sure you are, baby." She put her head on his shoulder. With murmurings and coaxings, she got him to put on his dinner jacket and smoke a cigarette while he waited for Mom to slip into her favorite blue cocktail dress.

He was in a worse mood now, though. "How was the movie?" he asked begrudgingly.

"Bogie in bandages," Mom said, waving a hand while she put on her lipstick.

"And how was the esteemed-in-his-own-estimation Peter Coleridge?"

"Cute kid," Mom said.

"He's a two-bit chiseler," Joe said. "I don't want him hanging around."

"C'mon, Joe, he's a kid."

"He's no kid, and I mean it. I knew him in the service. You, too, Evie. No puppy love crushes allowed on that sharpster."

Puppy love! I was so cheesed I couldn't speak.

Mom shrugged. "All right, Joe, but we can't avoid him completely. Tom invited him to our table for dinner tonight."

"I can't do anything about that," Joe said. "But as for you two, stay away from him."

I had always treated Joe as my dad. What he said stuck. He made the rules of the household.

It would be the first time I disobeyed him. And I would do it without even thinking twice.

Chapter 14

Mom looked so beautiful and glowy that I thought I'd be wallpaper, like I always was, but that night started something new. Mrs. Grayson waved and said, "Ooh la la, look at you. I know it's supposed to be girl–boy, but Evie, come sit next to me." Mr. Grayson told me I looked "very lovely this evening." He said it in a shy, courtly way that made me feel even prettier.

Peter stood up and pulled out a chair next to Mrs. Grayson, which meant he would be on my other side. Joe glowered as I sat down.

Peter leaned closer. "I guess I'm your boy, then, Evie," he said.

"And I'm your girl," I said right back.

There I was, right at the dinner table, in a grown-up dress. Candles were lit, the windows were open to catch the breeze, and everyone looked beautiful.

I was starting to catch the rhythm of the grown-up talk, how most things were a setup for a joke. And how people laughed at things even if they weren't funny, as long as they were said in a funny way. Joe had heard from somebody that there was a rumor that two German sailors had rowed to the beach from a submarine during the war. They'd had a drink at a bar and gone to the movies. Mrs. Grayson said people were way too afraid of spies and not afraid enough of politicians. That made everyone laugh. Peter said he was sure the story was true because everybody loved the movies, even Germans. Joe said we should have sent Lana Turner to Berlin and Hitler would have surrendered. Everyone laughed again.

His face flushed, Mr. Grayson held out an arm. "You see? Right here, at this table — this is how this hotel should be."

"Even on these awful chairs?" Mrs. Grayson asked. Everyone laughed, but I saw a line of worry between her eyebrows. There was a crease there that I was becoming familiar with, that you didn't see if you didn't look.

"With Joe and I running the place, it can't lose," Mr. Grayson said.

Silence fell on the table with a thud you could practically hear against your eardrums.

"What's this, Joe?" Peter looked from Joe to Mr. Grayson. "You two going into business together?"

"Tom?" Mrs. Grayson asked.

"Well, we need to do some research," Mr. Grayson said. "Spin down the coast, maybe to Miami, look at the hotels down there. Get a sense of things. But this place could be a gold mine. No question about that."

"So you're going in partners, Joe? That's great news," Peter said.

"Trust and a handshake," Joe said. "That's all a partnership is."

"And then there's the follow-through," Peter said.

"We should all move here!" I said. I tried to catch Peter's eye.

"Sure, why not," Mrs. Grayson said. "I love Palm Beach." She laughed, and it sounded like silverware ringing against a plate.

"I'm thinking about tennis lessons," Mom said.

"There's the ticket," Joe said. "That will keep you busy. Tennis, golf, whatever you want. You can play year-round in Florida, you know. Hey, let's order some champagne."

"There's a golf course in Lake Worth that's right by the lake," Peter said. "It gets breezy in the afternoons."

"That sounds like it's for me," Mom said.

We ate our chicken and our shrimp. Mrs. Grayson poured me a half-glass of champagne, and Joe didn't even mind. Mom had two glasses of champagne and glowed even brighter. Mrs. Grayson smoked instead of ate, and Mr. Grayson and Joe talked hotels.

"Let's have our coffee in the lobby," Mr. Grayson suggested, and everyone pushed back their chairs.

"Bed for me," Mrs. Grayson said brightly.

"Me, too," Mom said. "That champagne gave me a little headache."

"Mine is the size of Florida," Mrs. Grayson said, even though she hadn't touched hers.

"I'll come up with you, honey," Joe said.

"Don't be silly," Mom said. "Have your business talk with Tom. I'm taking two aspirin and going to bed."

I wandered after them into the lobby. Everyone seemed to have forgotten about me. When Peter said good-bye he barely looked at me. Tom and Joe picked a quiet corner, while Mom and Mrs. Grayson headed to the elevators.

I guessed Peter was being careful; he didn't want to get Joe steamed again. I felt lonesome, drifting around the lobby, too lonesome even for a game of solitaire.

In a few minutes I saw Wally come in and head for the desk. He was whistling under his breath, so I knew it was the end of his shift. I didn't want him to see me, so I ducked out of the lobby fast.

I killed some time doing what I used to do, walking through the hallways, peeking into the empty ballroom, looking for the fat man in the bar. Finally I slipped out a side door.

I breathed in the night air. Why did the air here smell like a pocketful of promises? It was the flowers and the ocean and the sky all mixed in together.

And then I saw Peter across the street, saw the gleam of his blond hair and the white of his jacket. The world seemed to fall away and arrange itself around him, and it was perfect.

He heard my clattering footsteps as I ran toward him, and he turned, surprised. "It's you, pussycat. What's the matter, can't sleep?" He took my hand. "Come on, let's go to the beach."

Perfect.

Chapter 15

A fat custard moon was splat in the purple sky, and a few stars were beginning to pop like fireworks. We left our shoes in the sand and walked down to the water. The baby waves lapped at our toes.

"Funny thing about the moon," Peter said. "When I was overseas, I'd look up at it, and I couldn't get that the same moon was over here, too. Everything happens underneath the same moon. Things you never thought you'd see. Or do."

I knew he was talking about the war, and I felt I shouldn't ask about it. So I kept quiet. I ducked my chin and looked up at him sideways, like Lauren Bacall in the movie we'd just seen.

But he wasn't looking at me. He was looking down the beach. "When I enlisted, I didn't know anything. What did I know? All I did was . . . play tennis, be a rich man's only son."

"But you have a brother."

"Oh, yeah. But the expectations were all on me. Dad wanted me to go into the navy — he nearly busted a gut when I chose the infantry. I got tossed into the worst of it right after basic training. Went from sweltering in basic to freezing my . . . well, freezing. All I knew how to do was march. Which didn't help me much. We didn't march in the Battle of the Bulge. We scrambled. I guess you read all about it in the papers."

"We didn't know Joe was in it until later. But we were scared he was." We'd known, even during the battle, how badly it was going. Nineteen thousand U.S. soldiers had been killed. *Nineteen thousand.* One of them had lived two doors down — William Armstrong, twenty years old. I remembered him as being the best whistler. Whistling "Chattanooga Choo Choo" as he walked by our house. Going to pick up his sweetheart, Rose Natalucci, on Saturday nights. The sound coming in my open window like a brass band, only it was just Billy Armstrong.

"Mud and snow and idiots. That was that."

"Did you meet Joe then?"

It was like he only just remembered I was there. "Hey, I'm not dumb enough to keep talking about the war with a pretty girl. Let's talk about you."

I shrugged, searching for something to say. *Every*

Young Girl's Guide to Popularity had always said to talk about the boy, not yourself.

"Tell me about home," he prompted. "Start there."

"Well, everybody's always in your business in my neighborhood. Everybody knows everybody, practically. And we live with Joe's mother. I'm supposed to call her Grandma Glad."

Peter snorted. "And she's a battle-axe, right?"

"How'd you know? Anyway, Mom keeps saying the house is too small now. So maybe we'll move. Maybe here," I said. "Since Joe and Mr. Grayson might buy the hotel."

Peter laughed softly. "Yeah, so I found out tonight."

"What's wrong with that?"

"Nothing, I guess. I don't get it, though. I thought Joe was selling those new washing machines."

"He's tired of it, he says."

"I wonder how much he's putting up."

"Nothing, he says. He's going to run it."

Peter shrugged. "I don't see what Grayson gets out of the deal. Or what a swanky couple like that is doing here in the off-season."

"I was thinking that maybe they're spies."

Peter laughed. "You've got some imagination, kiddo."

"It's just that . . . she's not happy, she just pretends. And he never talks about himself if he can help it. And she's always taking off alone. There's a big airbase here. Who knows what secret things they might be doing. She carries this big bag —"

"Full of spy stuff, right?"

"Well, what better cover would there be than owning a hotel? And I don't think she's very patriotic."

Peter nodded solemnly. "Definitely Commie spies."

He was treating me like a kid, which was definitely not a good thing.

"Do you ever think about moving here?" I asked. "Because of your father's business interests, I mean."

"Right. No, I haven't given it much thought. But maybe I should. Isn't that what your mother said, people need to start fresh?"

"That's just what I thought. I don't want to go home," I said.

He looked at me, smiling just a little. "Poor little bunny. Why is that?"

I forgot to tuck in my chin and look up, but it didn't matter.

"You're irresistible," he said. He leaned down and put his mouth on mine.

It was only a second. A quick kiss. He didn't even put his arms around me. But it was a kiss, a real kiss. Right on the lips. I felt his whiskery stubble against my chin. I was being kissed, and by a man, not a boy.

I understood the word *swoon*. It felt that way, like *sweep* and *moon* and *woo*, all those words smashed together in one word that stood for that feeling, right then.

"I shouldn't have done that," he said. "It's just that you looked so adorable."

"You didn't see me resist, did you?"

"That, my adorable one, is the problem. I don't mind being a heel occasionally, but I don't want to be a snake."

"You couldn't be a snake if you tried. Or a heel. You're a whole shoe. Laces and everything." I giggled, remembering my conversation with Margie. It felt so long ago.

"You're a nut," he said, smiling.

And he kissed me again, but it was on the tip of my nose, so it hardly counted. As a matter of fact, a kiss on the tip of the nose was probably *less* than a kiss.

"I wish a lot of things," he said, "and one of them is, I wish you were back in that house, with your battle-axe Grandma Glad."

It sounded like the most romantic thing anyone could say. As if we were falling in love, and we knew it was wrong, but we'd do it anyway. We'd follow our foolish hearts. We'd listen to the crazy moon.

Chapter 16

Our routine changed. Joe and Mr. Grayson took off in the late mornings and would be gone until cocktail time. Mrs. Grayson cycled off and went away for hours. Mom and I took our time dressing and sat in the lobby or out by the pool, pretending to be surprised when Peter would come by in his blue convertible and ask us if we felt like going for a spin. We knew that Joe didn't want us spending too much time with him, but neither Mom nor I really cared. Joe was so caught up in Mr. Grayson's world that he didn't have time to keep tabs on us.

It was a dreamy feeling, to drive along the ocean. The perfect blue of the sky meeting the blue of the sea, and every time I saw a palm tree it was a little shock, like life was yelling in my ear that this was me, and it was really happening.

Mom and I shared the front seat, which meant I got

to sit in the middle, right next to Peter. We'd listen to the radio, talking about the songs we liked, "Almost Like Being in Love" and "Put Yourself in My Place, Baby." Sometimes I forgot to be embarrassed and I sang along, really sang like I did when I was alone.

"You have a nice voice," Peter said. "Like Doris Day."

I sang "Sentimental Journey," just a little of it, and then I swung into "Winter Wonderland."

"What are you, crazy?" Peter asked, laughing. "It's a hundred degrees out."

"Evie has the prettiest voice," Mom said. "But she's too shy to solo in glee club."

"Gloria Pillson is the soloist," I said.

"She has no shame, that girl," Mom commented.

"I say, come October, Gloria Pillson is going to have new competition," Peter said.

But I didn't want to think about going back. I didn't want to think about anything but here. Joe was right. Florida could be a whole new beginning for all of us.

We drove to the docks and waited for the fishing boats to come in. Peter told us the names of Florida fish, oddball names like *pompano* and *sailfish* and *tarpon*. We sat on the beach and watched the surf casters and their long, looping lines snaking out over the breakers. We stopped at deserted beaches to swim.

One afternoon Mom put her hand on my arm as I started toward the water. "No, Evie. You just had a sandwich. You have to wait an hour."

Peter shook his head at Mom. "You believe all that stuff? Come on, Beverly. Evie's not a kid. I've been swimming in the ocean all my life. I can tell you, she's not going to drown if she just ate three bites of chicken."

"She's all I've got," Mom said. "I've got to watch out for my baby."

"Watch this, then." Suddenly Peter reached out and grabbed me by the waist. He flipped me over his shoulder. I felt the skin of his back against my cheek, warm from the sun, softness over tight muscle. I whooped as he walked to the ocean and tossed me in like I was a handful of nothing.

I surfaced, blinking the water from my eyelashes. Mom was yelling and running down the sand, but she was laughing. She looked like a teenager as she pretended to pound Peter on his bare chest. He scooped her up in his arms and swung her around. Then he threw her in, too.

"I think it's time Evie got a driving lesson," Peter said a few days later. It was a hot, muggy day, and we were all sleepy. Peter had driven west, past the city and into the country, with fields and farms.

Mom opened her mouth, but Peter reached past me and put a finger on her lips. "And don't say she's too young. You game, Evie?"

So with bumps and starts and with the car weaving all over the road and Mom laughing in the backseat, not minding at all, I learned to drive. Peter never looked scared, even when I'd head for a ditch. He'd just reach over, grinning, and put one hand on the wheel.

Afterward we stopped at a filling station for icy cold Cokes. They had two water fountains, one for Whites and one for Coloreds. I'd seen a few of them on the drive south. A Negro girl was taking a drink while her mother looked on. When the mother met my eyes, she quickly looked away.

Peter was watching, too. "You don't like seeing it, do you, pussycat?"

"I never thought about it before. But after you fight a war, you figure the world is going to get a little more fair, don't you?"

Peter waved his Coke bottle. "You take the whole world, it's all segregated. Between the haves and the have-nots. Down here the coloreds are lucky, in a way. They have signs. They can't make a mistake. The rest of us get it wrong all the time. We have to figure out how to break the rules."

I didn't believe Peter meant what he said. I didn't

wonder why a rich man's son would be so mean and feel so bitter.

I watched his throat as he took a long sip from the bottle. "But you can break the rules," I said. "They can't."

"Sure they can. Look at Jackie Robinson."

"Yeah, that's what people say when they want to stop an argument about the coloreds," I said. "It makes me feel sorry for Jackie Robinson. That's a lot for one man to do, on top of covering second base."

Peter shook his head. "You're good, you know that?"

"I'm not so good," I said.

"Don't shrug it off," Peter said. "It's better than mink, what you have."

"Nothing's better than mink," Mom said. She slung her arm around me. She kissed me on the temple, a certain place that only she knows. "Except Evie."

Then she put her hand out, her palm toward me. I put my palm against hers. We locked fingers.

"You and me," she said.

"Stick like glue."

"Just like Fred and Ginger do," we said together.

Peter smiled at us. "What's that?"

"We've been saying it forever," I said. "Through all the bad times."

"Bad times?"

"What, you think we haven't had any?" Mom challenged him, smiling, but her look was tough, like he'd gotten her all wrong and she didn't like it.

"Oh, I guess when Joe was away . . ."

"Well, sure, but before that," Mom said. "Late on rent day, getting kicked out of our apartment, no money for anything but a can of beans —"

"When I got scarlet fever —"

"And the doctor bills —"

"And then the worst time. When Aunt Vivian wanted to take me away from Mom and adopt me — Mom fought her like crazy. She even risked her job, and there were no jobs around back then."

"Nobody takes my baby away," Mom said.

"So what happened?" Peter asked.

"I prayed in church," I said.

"And God heard," Mom said. "He sent a miracle."

"Clue me in," Peter said.

"Aunt Vivian got pregnant," I said. "And she didn't want me anymore."

"That was a miracle?"

"You never saw Aunt Viv," Mom said pointedly.

Mom and I never said anything to each other, but we didn't have to. She knew and I knew that it was better not to mention our drives with Peter. We struck a bargain, but we didn't have to talk about it. After he dropped us off, I would at least pretend to do homework in the room. I did a lot of writing *Mrs. Peter Coleridge* in my notebook, which is exactly the kind of stupid behavior I used to roll my eyes at when Margie used to do it.

Mom took golf lessons, which proved to me how much a place can change you, because Mom's old idea of exercise was crossing her legs. "Who knew I'd take to golf?" she said. She grew tan and slimmer and blonder as the days went on. She'd come home laughing about her lousy score, her car plastered with orange petals. I'd watch from the window as she tossed her keys to Wally and ran up the stairs. I watched him soap the car down, washing it in slow circles, then stream water from buckets down it until it shone again. Sometimes if no one was around he'd take off his shirt and work bare-chested in the sun, and I was surprised at his tight, ropy muscles.

I don't know when it happened, but things started to turn, just a little bit, like when you smell the bottle of milk, and you know it's going to be sour tomorrow, but you pour it on your cereal anyway.

Joe was drinking more. Before dinner he'd have a drink or two before we went downstairs for cocktails. He didn't want to get the fish-eye from Grayson, he said, because Mr. Grayson only had one gin and tonic at night. He said that Mr. Grayson was dragging his feet and he didn't know why he put up with it. He asked Mom to spend more time with Mrs. Grayson, because he was sure she was putting the kibosh on the deal. He put off our return to New York again, and even had a shouting match long distance with Grandma Glad about it. Grandma Glad wasn't happy about Joe maybe starting a business in Florida.

"This is my chance, Ma!" I heard him yell. "Maybe this is my lucky day, did you ever think of that?"

Lucky days. That's what I thought. I had fistfuls of luck, and life was candy. I walked pretty, and I threaded a scarf through my belt loops and tied it tight to show off my waist. I didn't pay attention to Joe, or the Graysons. I counted each day as another day to spend with Peter.

Except that now I was tired of our drives, of Mom next to me on the seat. I wanted to see him alone.

Margie and I had memorized a poem in *Every Young Girl's Guide to Popularity*:

If in spite of your commands
Your Galahad has wandering hands
If on a date his lips do wander
Your virtue you must never squander
Your reputation is a shining prize

To guard it well you must be wise
If a girl is free with Tom, Dick, and Harry
Chances are she'll never marry.

Squandered virtue was a sin, Margie told me. But she had eight kids in her family. It seemed to me that her mother squandered her virtue all over the place.

Your reputation. What did that mean? Back home, it meant you couldn't go past first base with a boy. But here . . . I knew no one. No one could see. What was stopping me from finding out what lay behind Peter's kiss? He had kissed me that one time, a real kiss, right on the mouth. Sure, he'd regretted it, but he'd done it. He'd called me irresistible, so why was he resisting?

Then one night as I was falling asleep, I guessed it.

He was waiting for me to let him know I was ready.

Chapter 17

I could hear Joe's running footsteps in the hall before he swung open the door hard and looked at me.

"Where's your mother?" he asked.

"Playing golf."

"Come on, let's pick her up early." Joe walked in, picked me up, and swung me around. "The deal is going through. Tom made the offer, and it was accepted."

"You mean we're moving to Florida?"

"We're moving, kiddo! Nothing's been signed, but Tom and I shook hands on the deal."

"Wow!"

"We sign the papers on Wednesday. Come on, let's go spread the cheer. Tom said I could take the Cadillac." He grabbed my hand and we flew down the hall.

We jumped into the big beautiful car and Joe took off, driving down along the ocean, all the windows open. As we crossed the Lake Worth Bridge, the blue lake turned flat gray and the first drops began to fall. I heard a distant rumble of thunder.

Joe turned into the parking lot of the golf course. In front of us was a long rectangle of green that ran down the side of the lake. Golfers were pushing their carts toward the clubhouse, not hurrying too much yet in the cooling rain. We sat, waiting to see Mom, trying to spy the splash of pink of her blouse, or her white golf skirt.

I looked around the parking lot. Her car wasn't there. I was about to tell Joe, but I realized he'd already noticed. Still we sat in the car, staring at the wet grass, until every last golfer left the course and the thunder boomed.

She came in the front doors as Joe and I sat waiting. He wouldn't go upstairs, he wouldn't change, he just sat in the chair, feet planted. I wanted to wait for her out in the courtyard but he said, "Stay here, Evie," and that was that.

Mom smiled as she saw us, but something in Joe's face must have warned her, because she tossed her hair back in a way I knew well. When the rent was late, when she hadn't paid the milkman, she never got weasely, she got defiant.

Joe put down his drink and leaned back. "How was the golf game?"

She took another deliberate step forward and picked up his drink. She took a sip.

Arlene came through the door then, carrying her big canvas bag, and Mom put down the drink.

"Hello, troops," Mrs. Grayson said.

"I didn't go golfing today," Mom said. "I was with Arlene."

Arlene was wearing her sunglasses. We couldn't see her eyes. And if you weren't watching carefully, if you were, like Joe, keeping your eyes on your wife, you wouldn't have seen that she hesitated for a minute before she turned to Joe. "I found all the bargains, you'll be glad to hear," Arlene said to him. "Your wallet is safe, m'dear."

Arlene walked off to the elevator. Mom leaned over and kissed Joe. "Let me take a quick bath and I'll join you," she said. She slipped away, hurrying to catch the elevator with Mrs. Grayson.

"You didn't tell her," I said.

Joe leaned his head back and closed his eyes.

That night the voices woke me up. Arguing.

"Why ties, Bev?"

"Not this again."

"Why ties? Why not gloves? Why not dresses?"

"Oh, for Pete's sake. I told you, that's where they placed me."

"The tie department?"

"That's right, Joe." Her voice was so weary.

"You must have had a lot of customers."

He hit the last word with a hard *c* and let it roll out, *cus-to-mers.*

"Shhh! You'll wake the hotel!"

I slid out of bed and went to the louvered door, put my ear against it.

"Yeah," he continued. "Mom told me how well you did, how you sold more ties in a month than the poor slob you took over for did in a year."

"Not really. There was a war on —"

"Oh, you remember that, do you?"

I heard the sounds of them moving around, getting ready for bed. The slap of the hairbrush against the vanity.

"So you recalled you had a husband in the service, that's good."

"It's late. Let's go to sleep."

"And the candy store, Bev. Nice how your uncle took care of you."

"Yeah, it was lucky."

"Evie told me. Cut you plenty of slack, gave you extra

money on rent day. But then after he died, your aunt cut you off. Why do you think she did that?"

"Because she was a bitch."

"No reason, then."

"Dry up."

"No reason in the world."

"I'm going to bed."

"Right?" Joe's voice was loud now. I heard a crash, and Mom gave a little yell. I flung open the door.

The pineapple vase was on the floor, smashed. Mom bent down to pick up the pieces. I started forward, but she shook her head.

"Go to bed, baby." Her voice was calm but her hands shook as she stacked the pieces, bright yellow, bright green.

"No reason in the world." Joe muttered this, his back to me, and I heard ice hit a glass.

I woke up to the sound of my door opening. Four A.M. I sat up. Joe stumbled through the doorway, tripped on a sandal, and fell by my bed.

He cursed into the carpet. There was no Grandma Glad to say *None of that language, you're out of the army now, Sergeant.*

"Are you okay?" I whispered.

"Yeah." He turned over and lay faceup. "I love her. I love your mother. You know that."

"I know that."

"I didn't mean to break the vase."

"I know."

"I'm not sorry it broke, though. Damn, it was ugly."

Somehow Joe and I started to laugh. "It was just plain awful," I whispered.

Joe stared at the ceiling. "She's all I thought about, getting back stateside, doing right by Bev. Getting her things she never had. Taking care of her. She's my baby doll." In the dim light, I saw the silvery streaks of tears on Joe's face. "I'm all balled up, now. I'm just all balled up."

"Go to sleep."

It was warm in the room, but I slid off the bed and put a blanket over him. He caught my wrist and held it, his eyes closed.

"Where does she go, Evie?" he asked. "Where does she go?"

Chapter 18

To celebrate the sale, even though it hadn't happened yet, Mr. Grayson announced that he was taking us all to dinner down the coast. Even Peter.

It was time to wear the moonlight dress.

I wanted to make an entrance. Mrs. Grayson would say, I was sure, that the dress deserved an entrance.

I got dressed the way I'd seen Mom do it. Not just throwing on clothes, but walking back and forth between the mirror and the closet, brushing my hair, studying my face, sitting in my slip, smoothing the tiniest wrinkles from the skirt of the dress. Carefully, slowly, putting on lipstick. Watching myself in the mirror as I put powder on my nose and my bare shoulders. Perfume in my cleavage, the way I'd seen Mom do.

I'd mostly been just a kid during the war, and now that it was over, the only thing I wanted to remember was the romance of it. I didn't want to think of it like

Mrs. Grayson, that it gave the small-minded among us something to do. It made me think of Grandma Glad, pursing her lips over the success of her Victory Garden, refusing to give away her cabbages.

I wanted to think of music, of dances, of falling in love and getting married before he got shipped overseas. And the songs — *I'll be seeing you in all the old familiar places* — all that longing, all that waiting. It made sense to me now. Every lyric. It wasn't about just hearing it on the radio. The strings were stretched and quivering and going crazy inside me.

If Peter and I had met during the war, would we have gotten engaged? Would things have moved faster? I knew girls who were pre-engaged at school. I used to laugh at their smugness. Now I wanted it. Time rushed at me like a subway, all air and heat. I was afraid one day we'd all pack up our cars and drive away, and I'd lose him.

"You ready in there?" Joe bellowed.

"I'll meet you downstairs! I'm not ready!"

"Aw, criminy, Evie. Do me a favor. Don't turn into your mother."

I could see it in his face. Peter saw me, really saw me, and so did Mrs. Grayson and so did Mom and so did Joe.

"You look like a dream," Peter said.

"Where did you get that dress?" Joe bellowed the words, and the lobby went silent.

Mrs. Grayson moved forward and took my arm. "I bought it for her. Doesn't she look stunning?"

"Beautiful," Peter said. "She's all grown up."

"No, she's not!" The sharpness in Mom's voice made everyone freeze.

Joe came forward. He took my other arm. "Go upstairs and put something decent on."

"Joe, she's perfectly decent —" Mrs. Grayson started.

"I'm her *father*!"

Joe tugged me toward the elevator.

"She's almost sixteen," Mrs. Grayson said. But Mr. Grayson looked at her and she stopped talking.

Joe went on one side, Mom on the other. They steered me into the elevator and we went up to the room. I wanted to cry in great heaving gulps, in a way I hadn't cried in forever. But I didn't.

Mom went to my closet and got out my old best dress, the pink one with the lace on the collar. She unbuttoned the gown and got me out of it. She pulled the pink dress over my head.

"That's it," Joe said from the other room. "That's it, Evie. If you're sneaking around behind my back, it stops now."

Mom's fingers fumbled as she tried to zip up the dress.

"I won't have that man sniffing after my daughter!" Joe shouted. "Did you see the way he looked at her? Like a boy scout going for his merit badge in hound dog!"

Mom got the zipper up. She turned me around. She leaned forward and wiped my face with a wadded-up tissue. Which didn't make sense, because I wasn't crying. She was.

"It has to stop," she whispered. "Baby, it has to stop."

Joe's mood improved after three cocktails. At the restaurant he pounded Tom on the back and called him "buddy." His face was flushed red, and Mom started to stub out cigarette after cigarette. I had Shirley Temples and a big bowl of spaghetti. It was not a good combo.

It was supposed to be a celebration, but nobody was celebrating. They were just making noise, like Joe, or drinking, like Mom. Mrs. Grayson and Mom weren't talking. I thought it was maybe because of the dress. Mrs. Grayson ordered a gin and tonic and didn't drink it. Mom didn't eat.

Joe kept saying, "It's a night to remember!" but you knew everyone else would want to forget it the very next morning. Even Mr. Grayson didn't look happy. He ate his steak in big bites and tucked a napkin into his collar to eat his spaghetti. It made him look like a ten-year-old.

Peter gave me a wry smile when we sat down, but he didn't try to talk to me. Every bite of dinner, every moment, I wanted to grab his hand and run out the door. The dinner felt like the longest night, like the night the world would end.

"You know, we never went fishing," Joe said. "We should do that tomorrow. Hire a boat down at the dock, make a day of it."

Nobody looked too excited about that.

"What do you say, Tom?" Joe asked. "We'll pack a thermos of drinks, get Rudy in the kitchen to pack a hamper."

"I heard there's a bad storm out in the ocean," Mr. Grayson said.

"We won't be in the ocean. We'll stay in the lake."

"I get seasick on motorboats," Mrs. Grayson said. "Sailboats, I like."

"You just have to know how to handle them easy," Peter said. "I grew up on the water. Got my sea legs early."

"Aw," Joe said, "did your rich daddy buy you a widdle boat? Did he let you toot the horn?"

"Sure," Peter said. "I like to blow horns. Nice and loud, so everyone can hear."

This seemed to make Joe even madder. "Nobody invited you, Coleridge."

"I did," Tom said. "If we're going, we should all go."

"You see that, Joe?" Peter said. "Nobody likes being left behind. It makes you feel kind of itchy."

"So scratch."

Everyone looked at Joe and Peter. The wave of fury crashed and rolled back between them.

"Isn't the moon pretty?" Mrs. Grayson said.

Everyone smoked a cigarette with coffee after dinner, and then it was time to go at last. We all stood outside, waiting for the valets to get our cars. The dark palms whispered in a quickening breeze. I looked at Peter. He had his hands in his pockets and was looking at Mom and Joe.

Look at me look at me look at me look at me

The valet brought Mr. Grayson's car, and as everyone started to move toward it Peter was suddenly next to me. "What we need is a hurricane hole."

"A hurricane hole?"

"It's a place to leave your boat in a hurricane. You find a little cove and tie her up, let her ride out the storm. You and me should get ourselves a hurricane hole."

"Time to get rolling, Coleridge." Joe was right next to us now.

"I'm not good enough for your daughter, Joe?" Peter

133

asked. "Is that it? I'm not good enough to even talk to her? What else aren't I good enough for?"

Joe looked like he wanted to throw a punch.

And then Peter spoke so softly that only Joe and I could hear it. "Who's the dirty rat here, Joe? From where I'm standing?"

The two of them faced each other. Joe's face was closed up. His soft brown eyes had gone black and dull. I realized something for the first time: I'd gotten it all wrong. Peter wasn't afraid of Joe. Joe was scared of Peter.

Joe threw a punch. Peter stepped back and the fist didn't connect with a jaw or a nose, just Peter's ear, and not that hard. Joe staggered and almost fell, and this made him more angry. He looked like he was winding up for another one, but Peter stepped back, both hands up, palms out.

"I think it's time we called it a night, don't you, Sarge? Good night, Evie."

Peter quickly turned and walked across the parking lot. The Graysons and Mom had their backs to us while they got into the car. The valet was hurrying to get Peter's car, and Peter caught up to him and clapped him on the shoulder.

It had happened so fast that nobody had seen it but me.

Chapter 19

We pulled up at the hotel and Wally walked forward, almost casually. Usually he raced to get to the car door before you could open it.

"Here you go, young Walter," Mr. Grayson said, and gave him a quarter.

Wally didn't say anything. He just took the keys.

As we walked into the lobby, Mr. Forney the manager was standing there, as though he was waiting for us.

"Mr. and Mrs. Grayson, I need a word. Over by the desk."

It was the absence of *please*. Usually the guy pleased all over the place. *Please, sir, your messages. Please, sir, your dinner reservation is confirmed. Please step this way, sir, please.*

Just the way Wally had run out of yessirs.

I saw Mrs. Grayson's spine snap to. She looked over

at Mr. Grayson, but he stood, still with a pleasant smile on his face, not moving.

"How about right here?" he asked.

Joe moved closer, flanking Mr. Grayson. "Is there a problem?"

"You received a telephone message this evening," the manager said. "From a Mrs. . . ." he cleared his throat ". . . Garfinkle." He said the name like a wet tissue he was holding by a corner. "She requested that you call home. Something about a wire transfer of funds." He paused. "The lady in question claimed to be your mother."

Mr. Grayson took the message slip out of the manager's hand and turned away. "Thank you."

"I have to ask . . ."

Mr. Grayson whipped around so fast Mr. Forney had to step back. "Do you? Do you have to ask?"

"If, in fact, this lady is your mother."

"Last time I checked," Mr. Grayson said.

"Tom," Mrs. Grayson murmured. She touched his sleeve.

"I'm sorry, we do have a strict policy," the manager said.

"And that is?"

"Mr. Grayson, we trusted that you and your wife were

Gentiles. But from speaking to your mother, we believe this is not the case."

"You didn't ask."

"It is an established Palm Beach custom. I understand that your people are happier down in the Miami area. I'll send a bellhop up for your luggage."

Mr. Grayson's face flushed. "Are you kicking me out of this hotel?"

"We find that your booking was open-ended, and we have a large number of guests arriving soon."

"That's bull," Joe said.

"We here at Le Mirage strive for the comfort of all our guests, and they have a right to expect —"

"Tom." Mrs. Grayson tugged on his arm. "Let's go."

"Not tonight. I'm not driving out tonight and looking for a hotel in the dark."

"I'm sure I can recommend some motels."

Mr. Grayson stared Mr. Forney down. "We'll be gone before breakfast."

The manager held his gaze for a moment. Then he inclined his head slightly. "I think that will be acceptable." He walked away stiffly, as if he was the one with the right to be angry.

For a minute nobody said anything.

"Let's go, Tom," Mrs. Grayson said.

"You're not going to say it?" he answered dully. "You're not going to tell me that you were right?"

"Sweetheart," she murmured. There was so much lovely warmth in that word, it was a wonder he didn't turn to her, but he didn't, he just kept staring ahead.

"Tom," Joe said. "Is there anything we can do?"

Tom's mouth twisted. "Like help me pack?"

"This is terrible," Mom said. "I . . ."

But this moment was for the Graysons. Nobody else. Mrs. Grayson looked at Mom with a "butt out" look that even I could read.

So we just stood there and watched them push the elevator button. Watched them wait. Watched them get on. We didn't move a muscle.

Ugly. Once in the schoolyard Herbie Connell threw a rock and it hit me in the back. This felt like that, ugly hitting me in the back.

"Whew," Mom said as soon as the door to our suite closed behind us. "That crummy little pipsqueak manager. I should have stuffed that stupid bow tie down his throat."

"I can't believe this is happening to me," Joe said. "We're signing tomorrow. This is going to blow everything."

"How do you mean?" Mom asked. "They're getting kicked out of the hotel, not Florida. Why won't he sign the deal?"

"Did you see their faces? Don't you get it?" Joe said angrily. "The deal is off! Christ, Bev, can't you get anything?"

"It's not my fault," Mom said. "You get that, Joe? Everything is not my fault!"

Joe paced to the bed and back. "I've got to think."

"What's to think about? You'll talk to Tom tomorrow and get it straightened out."

"You think we can buy this hotel now, the two of us? Now that they know?"

"So buy another hotel! It doesn't have to be in Palm Beach. Who needs it, anyway?"

"And you weren't any help. Why did Arlene sour on you that way? Couldn't you help me out? What happened with her, anyway?"

"It didn't take you long. What was it, maybe thirty seconds? I knew you'd come around to blaming this on me. You knew the deal was risky. You knew he was Jewish, didn't you? That's why he needed your name on the deed."

"He was going to be a silent partner. Who would care?"

"They'd care! So maybe he wanted to bust this place wide open — I'm not saying he's wrong — but I'm saying, you shouldn't be surprised that it blew up, that's all. That's what happens when you try to fix things

139

sometimes. Things that the swells like just the way they are."

"So this is my fault."

"No, it's not your fault, Joe." Mom sounded tired. "But it's not mine, either. You never tell me the real deal. You screw up, it's my fault. I want to make my own screwups, thank you."

"Oh, you're plenty good at screwing, dollface," Joe said. "That's clear."

"Stop fighting!" I yelled. But they didn't stop.

"Why'd you marry me, Joe? Why'd you ask me to marry you?"

"I thought different then."

"You didn't trust me then, though, did you? You never did, but I didn't want to see it. I thought it was because you loved me so much. But no, you made sure I had a chaperone while you were overseas. Your mother, watching me like a hawk. So if I stopped to buy a pack of gum, she'd want to know what I was doing for those five minutes."

"Did you need a chaperone, Bev?"

"Stop it," I begged. "Please, stop it."

"You must have met a lot of fellows, selling ties."

"Stop it!"

I wanted to put my hands over my ears. I was gulping my tears into my mouth. I didn't want to hear any more ugly tonight. So I ran.

Chapter 20

I ran down the streets barefoot, sandals in both hands, hiccupping my misery into the air. Past The Breakers, down a street lined with palm trees, turning again.

It was so dark. The moon was behind the clouds. The tall ficus hedges on either side of the road were like giant men in a fairy tale, scary and mean. I ran and ran on the dark silent street. All the houses were shuttered, their owners away until winter, when the island would come alive. What a screwy place, I thought, when you had to wait until December to wake up.

I kept thinking about Tom Grayson's hand squeezing that piece of paper. And the manager's face. He had been waiting to deliver that news. He had been *happy* to do it. That was the ugliest part.

And Joe and Mom. I'd heard them fight, but never like that, where they wanted to say the meanest things they could, the cruelest things they could think of.

I needed someone to explain it to me. Someone who would tell me the real deal.

I remembered the blue convertible turning down a street, and that's where I headed. There were no cars anywhere, no lights on in the houses. I walked and walked, down one street, then another. The driveways curved away from the street, and I had to run down each one to look for the car. I pressed my face against garage-door windows.

Finally I noticed a dirt road under a canopy of pines. It was solid dark, too dark to see anything but the outline of a white house shaded by tall trees with twisted roots. The shutters were drawn tightly over the windows. I went alongside the house, down a narrow crushed-shell driveway. It hurt my feet, so I put my shoes back on.

The blue car was pulled up underneath the overhanging branches of a tree. A breeze sent the branches shivering, and a shower of orange petals fell on my head. It seemed like a good omen. I walked into the backyard.

He was sitting outside. Two chairs, chaise lounges, angled toward each other. Peter was sitting on one, in the dark, staring at the swimming pool, empty and clogged with debris. Leaves and grass and sand had collected in the bottom, rotting and brown.

"Checking up on me?" he asked, his back to me. "How considerate."

He didn't sound glad.

I walked closer, and he turned. Whatever expression was on his face was gone in less than a moment. "Well. Hello, you."

Now that I was here, I didn't know what to say. "It's so gloomy. Why don't you turn on a light?"

"They turn off the electricity in the summers. They told me to turn everything on, but I don't want to impose. I told you I was camped out."

"The windows are all boarded up."

"In case of hurricanes. I didn't want to ask the caretaker to take them down. The guy looks about ninety. What's wrong?"

"I just had to see you."

"Don't fret, pussycat. The punch didn't hurt."

"No, I mean, I'm sorry about the punch, but — the Graysons got kicked out of the hotel. Tonight. They're Jewish. The manager just kicked them out, just like that."

Peter let out a *ppphhhh*, shaking his head. "Palm Beach is restricted. You know that."

"I didn't know. Anyway, you can't just kick someone out like that."

"Of course you can. That's the way it works. I told you that before. They just didn't have a sign outside, but

Arlene and Tom knew what could happen if they tried to pass. What are they going to do?"

"They're leaving in the morning. Peter, you don't understand," I said. "The manager. He *enjoyed* it."

Peter sighed.

"I don't get it!"

"That's a good thing," he said. "A good thing that you don't get it."

"But you do. You get it. So clue me in. Tell me how someone could do that and be happy about it!"

"Baby, I was in a war. Of course I get it. That's where all the bad in the world *comes* from. Guys who like being mean." Peter's face went tight and closed. "I was that guy once. So was Joe. We were all that guy, for at least a minute. We had to be."

I felt the close, hot darkness around me. "Tell me what you did. Tell me," I said, very slowly, because just then I realized it, the whole obvious truth of it right in front of my face, "what you and *Joe* did. Together. What happened? You say I'm good. I don't need good. I need to *know* things. I need to know why Joe drinks so much, and why he hates you. Why he wants to move here. Why he wants to get away."

"Ask him. He's your dad."

"Tell me. Tell *me*, Peter. Tell *someone* and let it be me."

144

He jerked his face away, looked down at the empty swimming pool.

He looked so wretched that it made me brave. "Tell someone who loves you," I said.

"You don't love me, kiddo," Peter said softly. "You're a lovely little girl with a lovely little crush. You don't know me —"

"I do know you. I know you right down to the ground," I said. "I know that you were nice to Mr. Grayson when he was embarrassed about being 4-F. I know that night I met you that you felt sorry for me, that you knew how stupid I looked in that gown and you danced with me anyway. I know you taught me to drive because you wanted me to have a piece of being an adult. You saw that Mom treated me like a baby, and you showed her that I wasn't. I know that you didn't punch Joe tonight because he was drunk and you would have flattened him. I know that whatever you did, however bad it was, that *you're* not bad."

He stood there, and I saw something change for him. I saw *me* change for him. That dress I thought had changed me in his eyes? It had been nothing. This was it, this was finally it, when I got what I wanted.

He sat down at the edge of the pool, his feet dangling. After a minute I sat next to him.

"In the infantry," he said, "you walk and walk through

miles of broken things. Trees snapped in two. Bridges cut in half. Walls of farmhouses blown away so you see chairs and a kitchen table with a cup sitting on it, dusty and perfect. And then there are the things you see that you stop thinking about even while you're walking by them. You've got you and your squad and that's it. You can't even remember home anymore, even though you tell your buddies about it. You get used to lifting stuff from another outfit if you need it. A wrench, a gun, some rations — a Jeep, even. Everybody did it. War turns you into a crook and a liar and a cheat. Except you never cheat your buddies."

Peter put his hands on both sides of his body, as if he wanted to push himself off and leap into the pool. "You remember the story from when you're a kid, about Aladdin's Cave?"

"Sure."

"Well, we found it, Joe and me. After the war. It was a warehouse in Salzburg. Filled with loot. Treasure. And it belonged to nobody. This train, it left Hungary near the end of the war, packed with stuff. The Germans tried to hide it. Only we got our hands on it. It was things that belonged to the Jews. Everything you could imagine. Dishes and rugs and watches and rings and paintings and silverware. You name it. And it was all loaded into this warehouse until they decided what to do with it."

"What happened . . ."

"To the Jews? I don't know. Most of them were dead, I'm sure. Sent to the camps. Maybe some of them made it out; it was near the end of the war. Maybe some were DPs, but how were we supposed to trace them?"

DPs. Displaced persons. No home to go back to. No city, no town, no country even.

"Anyway, there were crates and crates of this stuff. And the people who owned it were probably dead. Name after name, they had, the Germans. They kept track of who owned what, down to every last spoon. But so what? Where was it going to go? Joe and I became buddies — he was the property officer, see — and one night we said to each other, Who's going to miss a bit of this, a bit of that?"

"So you stole it." I thought I wanted to know everything. But I didn't want to hear this.

"It wasn't just us. The officers took rugs and silver for their quarters. Joe saw it going out the door, and if some of it got shipped home, nobody seemed to care. Not then, anyway. We figured an easy way to get it out, just a couple of boxes of stuff, but good stuff, you know? And Joe knew about this suitcase full of gold. Gold dust. And what were we going to do, just let the army take it? By this time, you see, we were thinking about going home, and what we were going back to. The plan was,

Joe would get the gold stateside, and this guy he knew would help him get us cash for it and take his cut. Then, when I got sprung, we'd split the rest. But what happened was, Joe got home and didn't want to sit on the cash, waiting for me to get back. So he takes it all and buys a business. And then another one."

"He said it was a GI loan."

"After a while I'm writing him, and he's not answering. So as soon as I get stateside, I look him up. He dodged my calls. He didn't have the cash to give me. And then he takes off for Florida . . ."

"That was you who called that night."

Peter nodded. "And the next day I went over to your house, and your grandma might be a battle-axe, but if you talk to her right she brags about her son and how he's vacationing in Palm Beach. So off I go."

"Is Joe trying to cheat you?"

"Let me put it this way: I think he'd be a hell of lot happier if I disappeared."

"I don't get it. Your father is rich. Why do you need the money so bad?"

"Yeah, well, I didn't say I got along so well with dear old dad. And a deal's a deal. Now he's telling me that if he swings this deal with Grayson he'll be able to raise some cash and pay me off. He says he took most of the risk, so I can wait. But I get nervous waiting."

"If the Graysons knew what Joe did . . ."

"Yeah, they wouldn't be quite so friendly, would they? Going into business with a guy who steals from Jews."

I sat there, thinking about a warehouse full of stuff. Like that missing wall, when you could see into a farmhouse, tables and chairs and an empty cup. And all the stuff belonged to families. I looked down at the thin gold bracelet on my wrist, the one I never took off. I took it off and turned it over in my fingers. I wondered about the girl who'd owned it, who had to put it in a pile and give it to a German officer.

And then suddenly, for some reason, I thought of Margie stepping on the back of Ruthie Kalman's shoe.

"The thing is," Peter said, "over there, it was easy. We didn't think too much about it, we just saw our chance and took it. But lately I'm thinking crazy stuff. I'm thinking, there's a curse on that money. Maybe somebody has to pay."

We sat for a while and didn't say anything. I knew this moment was important. I knew I had to help him somehow. I couldn't make the pieces fit in my mind, about what I thought he was and what he did. But I knew I still loved him. I loved all the parts of him, even the ones I didn't understand.

I spun the bracelet around on the concrete. It made a little pinging noise. It rolled away and hovered on the edge of the empty pool for a minute. Peter and I both watched it fall in. It didn't make a sound.

"You know what the priest says in confession?" I asked him. "At the end, after you unload all your lousy sins? *I absolve you*, he says. I mean, he says it in Latin, and maybe he's bored and maybe he mumbles, but we know what he means and we believe it. You get a whole bunch of grace, and you get to start over. It's a good system if you think about it."

"Could you do that for me?" Peter asked.

"I absolve you," I said. I leaned over and kissed him on the mouth. I felt my breath mingle with his.

Our faces were so close. His eyes were soft, and he shook his head. Not to say no, but in a wondering way.

"Could it really happen like this?" he asked. "That a girl like you can make me feel . . ."

"Make you feel what?"

"Make me feel," he said.

I felt myself expand, as if the night had filled me up full of stars.

He stood up. "Come on," he said. "I'd better take you back."

I took his hand, and he pulled me up. I used the momentum to lean against him.

For once, he didn't put any distance between us. He took his hand and ran it down my spine. "You know what you have?" he asked. "True north."

"I don't know what that is."

He kept his hand on the base of my spine. "Inside you, right here, along your backbone . . . ," and he ran his finger down it again, making me shiver, ". . . you've got something. Like the needle of a compass. You know the right way to go."

He looked down at me, right into my face, and this time I got it. I got how to say *yes* without opening my mouth. He kissed me.

And the kiss turned into something deep and secret.

His mouth opened, and mine opened, too. His tongue went into my mouth and I was so surprised, I didn't know what to do. At first. Then he showed me.

My pulse seemed to have escaped its usual place. It was somewhere else now, beating in a deep secret place I didn't know was there. He placed his hand on the small of my back, as if we were dancing, and held me tight against him.

Then he stumbled against the chaise and landed on it. He went backward, and I was on top of him. He kept his arms around me, and we kissed again, even deeper, with need driving it this time.

151

I knew this was wrong, and I knew I didn't care, but I was confused. No one had gone through the *steps* of this with me. I only had Margie in my head, nodding knowingly even though she didn't know anything.

He pushed up against me, against my skirt. This was it, this was the knowing.

I didn't want to stop, but I needed a breath. I pulled away, just a little bit.

"Okay," he said. His breath was short. "Okay, baby, we'll stop."

"No, I never want to stop —"

"Evelyn!" The voice was a shout.

Mom stood just a few feet away. "Evelyn, get up."

I'd seen her mad at me before, of course. *Close the door, can't you feel that draft? Do you expect me to pick up after you all the time? If I say come home at nine o'clock, that means nine o'clock, not twenty minutes after!*

This was different. Her face seemed thinner, white, her eyes dark.

I slid off Peter's lap.

"Bev —"

"Don't speak to me." Mom spit out the words. "Either of you."

"How did you find me?" I asked her.

"It's not what you think, Bev," Peter said. "She —"

"I love him!" I said. "I love him! It's not terrible, what I did. I love him and he loves me!"

"Evie, get in the car." Her voice was spooky. So tight, so shaky.

"I love him!"

"Beverly —"

She picked up an ashtray and threw it.

I don't know whether she was aiming at me or him.

It hit the concrete and sprayed glass at me. A piece cut my forehead, near my eye.

"Christ!" Peter took a handkerchief from his pocket and dabbed at my cut. I could feel the blood running down the side of my face. He looked at me frantically. "Christ, Beverly!"

I didn't care because he was looking at me with such concern. *He loves me. He loves me, he does, he does!*

"Get in the car," Mom said again. "Right now. Get the hell out, I mean it!"

I could have fought her. I could have taken what I knew about what he felt and thrown it at her, proved I was an adult now, just like her. But feeling grown up? I discovered something right then: It comes and it goes. I was still afraid of my mom.

I walked past her. I left her there with Peter.

I walked to the car. It was parked snugly next to Peter's,

153

underneath the tree. I started toward the passenger door and stopped as a sudden strong breeze shook the tree and orange petals showered down. They fell softly on the hood like a blanket.

I scooped up some petals and crushed them in my fist. What was I going to do?

Mom had been paying attention all along. She knew how I felt about Peter. She knew exactly where to find me tonight. And now she'd tell Joe. I would never see Peter again if they had anything to say about it. They'd keep me a little girl in my pink dress forever if they could. They'd refuse to see what Peter had seen in me tonight.

But how grown-up could I be if I couldn't defy her? Why couldn't I run back and stand up to her?

I leaned against the car. I could just see my face in the reflection of the windshield. I could see it like a smudge on the window. I wanted to smash the scared little girl I saw there. Who was I more angry at, Mom or myself?

She ran up to the car, wrenched the door open, and I got in. I slid over to the passenger side, all the way up against the window, and she followed. She took off, tires spinning in the shells, reversing back down the driveway, and then heading for the hotel.

She drove fast with all the windows open. My cut

stung and I felt blood running down the side of my face. I tasted it.

"Oh, Evie," she said. "Don't be a fool like me."

She pulled into the hotel parking lot and set the brake. She rested her head on the steering wheel. Then she straightened and tilted the mirror toward her. She slowly put on lipstick, making her shaking fingers cooperate.

Then she got out and slammed the car door. She smoothed her hair and her skirt, waiting for me before we went into the hotel.

"I'm not going to tell Joe," she said.

I looked at her, surprised.

"This will have to be our secret. And it can't happen again. It's already gone too far."

I wanted to tell her there was no going back. But what was the use?

"Never again," she said. "Promise me."

There was only the sharp sound of our heels on the pavement, filling up the silence between us. She had asked for my promise, and I hadn't given it. But she didn't ask for it again.

Chapter 21

Someone had left a raft floating in the pool. It kept bumping up against the rail near the steps. I thought maybe I could sleep on it. I took off my sandals and bunched up my skirt in one hand and went in and grabbed it, hoisted myself up. Water sloshed over the side and got my skirt wet. I pushed off from the side.

I wanted to stain this place, leave my mark after this night. I hoped my blood would fill up the pool, but it drifted away, a skinny ribbon of pink.

I floated for a long time. I found out that without sun, you don't get sleepy on a raft. You just get wet.

Then over my head I saw Mrs. Grayson looking down at me. She was dressed in a skirt and flat shoes, a handbag over her arm.

"What are you doing out here?" she asked.

"I couldn't sleep."

"So what are you doing in the pool, counting sheep?"

I raised myself up and started to paddle toward her.

"Tom's packing the car."

"I thought you were staying until morning." I climbed out, dripping.

"The bed's not as comfortable as I thought." She stubbed out her cigarette and regarded it for a minute. Then she flicked it into the pool.

We were quiet for a minute, just watching the cigarette stub float. She had a sweater around her shoulders and she hugged herself and shivered, even though it was warm. I'd never seen her without lipstick on before. Ladies' mouths look so pale and small without lipstick.

"There's a storm coming. We heard it on the radio." Mrs. Grayson said this absently, looking off toward the ocean we couldn't see, a block away. "A hurricane. Supposed to hit south of us, near Miami."

"We didn't know the hotel was restricted," I said.

"Every Jew knows about Palm Beach. It's on the deeds to the houses, you know. No Negroes, no Jews."

"I don't understand. Why did you come?"

"Well, I guess the best way to say it is, Tom wanted to get away from everything he was, and this is as far as you can get."

I was suddenly so tired. I wanted to sit down, but I didn't want her to think that I didn't want to talk to her.

"I thought you might be spies," I said.

She grunted a laugh. "Maybe we were."

"Why does he want to get away?" I asked.

She didn't say anything for a minute. She noticed the cut on my forehead. "What happened to you?"

"I ran into something tonight," I said.

"Do you know what Yom Kippur is?" she asked, and after I shook my head, she said, "It's a holy day for us, the Day of Atonement. Tom was 4-F, but the war left its mark on him, too. On Yom Kippur last year, he just . . . went to the movies. He wouldn't stay with us. He said it standing in his mother's living room. 'Atone?' he said. 'For what he did, God should atone to *me*.' You should have seen his mother's face. Poor Elsa."

"What did God do to him?"

"Killed his cousins," she said. "Samuel was like a brother to him. Sam's wife, Nadia. And Irene, their daughter. She was just your age. She had your same birthday, October thirty-first."

"What happened to them? To Irene?" I pronounced it like she had — *Ee-wren*. So much prettier that way. And I could see her, this girl I didn't know. Not her face, but her. I could see her lying on a bed on her stomach, her ankles crossed, listening to the radio. Just a girl like me.

"We tried to get them out, all of them. We didn't know what happened to them until after the war. A family friend contacted us, someone who made it through the camps, who knew what happened."

A girl with my birthday died in the camps. A girl I didn't know. I could see her on the bed, swinging her feet to a tune on the radio. I couldn't see her taken away. I couldn't see what happened after that. I knew about the camps, but I hadn't really thought about them. I'd seen the articles, but we'd had so much of war. I hadn't wanted to think about it after it was over, after all the men were coming home. I hadn't wanted to listen to the whispers about Ruthie Kalman's cousins. I didn't want any more of the war. I was sick of the war. I had wanted to listen to Joe saying, *It's over, over there, and here is where it's happening now.*

"So where will you go?" I asked.

"Home. We're going to drive home."

"I don't understand any of it," I said. "Why they won't let you stay. Why any of this can happen. I mean, we just fought a whole war."

"It wasn't about the Jews, kiddo," Arlene said softly.

"Joe is so angry. He says he's going to talk to the manager in the morning —"

"Sure. That's swell. But he's staying, right? He's not checking out."

I was quiet. The idea of checking out hadn't occurred to him. Or Mom. Or me.

"I'm glad you saw it, Evie," she said. "It's a good thing for someone like you to see."

"Why? I hated seeing it! It made me sick!"

"That's exactly why. Do me a favor?" She gave me a piece of paper, folded twice. It was a letter written on the back of a page torn from a calendar. Because I bet they wouldn't even use the hotel stationery now. "Give this to Joe. It's from Tom."

"What does it say?"

"What Joe already knows. Tom's pulling out of the deal. We have to go home now." She smiled and leaned over to kiss me. "It was nice getting to know you a little bit, Evie Spooner."

Our faces were very close. "You be careful now," she whispered. "Or better yet, go home. It's time for us all to just go home."

Chapter 22

In the morning Joe got up and left early. I heard the door click shut, and it was just beginning to get light. I heard a car engine start through the open window. After another minute or so, Mom crawled in bed with me.

She didn't say anything. She pulled me to her and kissed my temple, right in her secret spot. Then she held me, my head on her shoulder. We just lay like that, not talking.

Then finally she spoke. "One thing I was always happy about, Evie. I was happy you grew up plain, all knees and elbows. You weren't some curly-headed doll. It meant you'd use your brain. And you did. I wanted to keep you that way for as long as I could. When you started getting pretty, I didn't want you to know it. I was just watching out for you, you see, the best I could. You've got to understand something. Mothers don't want their kids to make their mistakes."

"Your mistake was what? Being pretty?"

"Maybe liking it a little too much. And finding myself in trouble."

In trouble. I didn't get it at first. I thought maybe she was talking about detention at school.

"You mean ... you were pregnant when you got married?"

She nodded. "I thought you figured that out a long time ago."

Who, me? Sister Mary Evelyn?

"Your father had to marry me. Uncle Bill made him. Oh, I don't know, I guess he loved me, in his way. But I loved him different. I loved him like a fever. Then he left. He kicked through love like it was dust and he kept on walking. So I had to raise you alone — and let me tell you, it wasn't easy. Because I was pretty. I had a kid and no husband, and people's minds get dirty. The men look and the women talk and it doesn't matter how straight a line you walk. It makes you so ... tired."

Before Joe, if she had a date, she said good night with the door open. She'd never let them in. She had some boyfriends, but nothing took. "One louse after another," Mom used to say. "I'm being choosy this time."

I had always loved my neighborhood. I loved that I knew all the shop owners, that Mr. Gardella in the candy store would toss me penny candy if my pockets were empty, that if Mr. Lanigan was heading home and had change in his pocket he'd buy me an egg cream. Beverly Plunkett's kid got egg creams and candy, and I always thought it was because I didn't have a father. Or was it because they liked looking at my mom?

"Joe was a good bet for us, sweetie. I saw it right away. I thought, here is a place to rest. Make a real life. Pot roast and potatoes, church on Sundays."

"Did you ever love Joe?" I asked.

"Sure, baby," Mom said. "But not as much as you did."

Joe came back, and we all went down to breakfast, like usual. We sat at the table we always sat at. It was almost like being a family. Except for the no talking part.

Joe's coffee cup rattled in its saucer. The lifeguard fished Mrs. Grayson's cigarette out of the pool. A breeze ruffled the palm trees and the napkins on the tables.

I tried to remember what it had felt like before we left. The steamy kitchen, both of us on Joe's lap, him offering the trip, the sense that the road was right outside the door and he would take us on it and it would be adventure and fun and everything he promised.

The letter sat in the pocket of my skirt. Some of the ink had run, but you could still read it.

Sorry to pull out like this. Look me up in New York.
Maybe we can get something going in a place
we know something about.

At the bottom was the name of the hotel, the Metropole, and an address on West Forty-eighth Street. If I gave it to Joe, I knew what would happen: We'd be packing up the car that morning, following the money. I couldn't let that happen. I had to find a way to make it all work. I had to get around Joe and Mom and show Peter that I was the one for him. He'd known it last night, even if it was just for a second.

I had to fix Mom and Joe. I'd done it before. The fights they'd had, even before they married, I could always fix them. Everybody had to go to the places they belonged.

I knew that last night Peter had come close to telling me he loved me. I could feel it in the way he'd said *Okay, baby, we'll stop.* I saw it in his face when he protected me from Mom.

Joe noticed the small cut on my head.

"What happened to you?"

"Bumped it."

Mom met my eyes over the coffee cup.

The door to the courtyard opened, and Peter walked in. He was exactly the last person I expected to see.

I stood up. I thought, right then, that he'd come to see me.

He said hello and held out my chair again, then pulled up one for himself. He raised a hand to the waiter for coffee. His hair was brushed straight off his forehead, his pale blue shirt open at the neck.

He seemed completely relaxed as he added cream to his coffee. "Good morning, all," he said. "I came to say good-bye to the Graysons, but Wally tells me they checked out. I think it's time I took off, too."

Mom slipped her dark glasses out of her purse and put them on.

"Tom told me I should look them up in New York," Peter said. He took a sip of coffee. "Now that I've got old times to talk about with them."

What had happened? Peter was leaving? I tried to figure this out.

Was he threatening Joe? Even though he said things so nice and easy. *Old times* — did that mean he'd spill the beans to the Graysons? For what? Spite?

Or was it absolution?

Was it because of what I'd told him last night?

Did that mean it was my fault if Joe lost the deal, if Peter went away?

I needed more time with Peter. If he told the Graysons, Joe would never let him in the door

165

again. There had to be another way to make things right.

We had to leave today, too. I could figure things out on the way up to New York.

I reached into the pocket of my skirt and took out the letter. "Oh, Dad, I forgot to give you this. Mrs. Grayson gave it to me."

"You forgot?" Joe grabbed the letter from me and read it quickly. "Well, there you go. That Grayson is a stand-up guy. We can still make a deal somehow."

"That's good, Joe," Peter said. He leaned back in his chair. "I'll tell him you said that when I see him. I'm taking off right after breakfast."

"We should all go home," I said. "Right, Joe?"

"What?" Joe said. "And miss the fishing trip?"

Peter's surprise made him jerk slightly back in his chair, like he was the fish on a line.

"Joe?" Mom said.

"I already talked to the kitchen — they made a hamper, chicken sandwiches."

"But the Graysons are gone," Mom said.

"So? We're going to pass up a trip because of that? After all, Pete is leaving. We don't want to leave without a fishing trip."

"No, thanks," Peter said. "I'm all gassed up and ready to go."

166

"You're not still sore about last night, are you, buddy?" Joe asked. "You're not the type to hold a grudge, are you? I was a little tight. I'm laying off the Scotch from now on, let me tell you."

"I'm not going," Mom said. "I have a headache."

"It's a nice breezy day. We'll have a ball. Won't we, Pete? You're the sailor, am I right?"

Peter didn't say anything. It was the first time I'd ever seen him look unsure.

"Come on, it's all arranged. I talked to Wally — his dad has a boat for hire. I'll drive us down to the dock."

"Joe —"

"No wet blankets allowed," Joe said, cutting Mom off. She clammed up.

I waited to see if Joe wanted me to come, too. I saw that he was in charge. Everyone was a little afraid of him, a little afraid of his mood. Even Peter.

"Evie can stay here, do her homework," Joe said. "Just us three today."

"All right, Joe," Peter said slowly. "If that's the way you want it. I'm game."

We all drove down to the dock together, even though it was within walking distance. The wind was stronger now, ruffling the gray water in the lake. It didn't seem to be the best day to take out a boat. I noticed that men were tying up their boats, not taking them out. Joe stopped at a dock with a sign. CAPTAIN SANDY, BOAT FOR HIRE. It was a white boat with a small cabin. A compact man in a cap was coiling rope on the deck.

"Permission to come aboard, captain," Joe said.

"I don't know about this," the man said. His legs were planted wide on the deck as the boat rolled. He tipped his chin toward a flag on a flagpole. "Small craft warnings. The harbormaster wants us to stay in port. Sorry Wally sent you down here for nothing."

"I'm not asking for a rowboat," Joe said. "Just your pretty little cruiser there."

Wally's dad shook his head. He had a big face with gray stubble, and his gaze was clear as he sized us up. I couldn't see Wally in him at all. "Find another boat."

"Come on, chum, we only want it for a couple of hours, tops. Give us a break, we're leaving tomorrow. Wally said you'd be glad to do it." Joe reached into his pants pocket and took out a bill. I couldn't see how much it was. He slipped it into the guy's shirt pocket.

"You know anything about boats?" Wally's dad asked.

"I do," Peter said. "I can handle her fine."

"We'll be back by two, three at the latest," Joe said.

"Maybe sooner," Mom said.

"Stay in the lake," Wally's dad said. "The inlets out to the ocean can get tricky in weather like this. Don't try it."

"Wouldn't think of it," Joe said. He reached into his back pocket for his wallet as the captain began to load the boat with some fishing gear.

Mom looked out at the water. "I don't know about this, Joe," she said.

"We'll have a ball," Joe said. "Here, Captain Sandy, let me give you a hand."

"It will be okay," Peter said to Mom. "I grew up around boats. It's not bad yet. We won't stay out long."

Mom looked seasick, and she was still standing on the dock. "It's better not to argue with Joe," she said, not so much to him, but to me.

Looking out at the whitecaps, I was suddenly scared. "Don't go," I said.

"It's going to be okay, pussycat," Peter assured me. "Trust me. This could be just what we all need."

I looked into his eyes. Maybe he was right. Maybe he could win Joe over, or they could make a different kind of deal. Maybe he could show Mom that she could trust him. Maybe they could come back a little more friendly than they were right now.

The three of them went aboard. Joe first, Mom next, settling herself nervously in a chair at the back. Peter got the bowline and jumped aboard. He saluted me.

He lifted a hand in good-bye. "We'll be back, Evie!" he shouted. "We'll be back!"

Chapter 23

"**B**ig storm coming," Wally said.

I stared at the pool. I wished he'd go away.

"Hurricane. They're thinking it might hit us. Or maybe south of here. Miami if we're lucky."

It was hard to believe. The wind had picked up, but there was blue sky overhead.

"Did your folks take out my dad's boat?"

I nodded. "Just for a couple of hours, though. They'll be back."

"So you're on your own for a while. I just got off."

He had brown eyes and was tanned, with freckles across his nose. He needed a haircut. His chest was slender, his skinny legs ending in large sneakered feet. I wondered if I could ever be interested in boys again.

But, as Joe sometimes said about women, the basic equipment was there, even if Wally didn't know what to do with it. Was there something I could learn from him, something I could take back to Peter, that knowledge I'd almost gotten last night?

I saw wanting in Wally's eyes. Now I could recognize it as easy as Margie waving at me across Hillside Avenue. What would happen if I got hold of that want and rode it like a raft to see where it could take me? Joe had left me behind like a kid. I didn't want to be a kid.

Anger built up behind my eyes. I kept thinking of Peter's kiss, so long and deep. What happened after the kiss? Sure, I knew the birds and the bees, but I needed more. I needed *practice*.

"Do you want to go for a walk?" Wally asked. "Look at the surf?"

I nodded.

No one was on the beach. The wind sent the sand stinging against our legs. The green water was pounding the shore. We walked past where the hotels were, back where the shuttered mansions faced the sea from behind the dunes. Wally picked a spot between two high dunes, a place where we'd be sheltered.

"What will happen if the hurricane comes here?" I asked.

"Depends. If it's a big one, they'll evacuate the island. They take people to the courthouse over in West Palm. I've been through hurricanes before — it's not too bad."

"You're just being brave. Boys are braver than girls." I said this without shame. I looked up at him sideways and saw him swallow. *Be dumb!* Margie always scolded me. *It works!*

I trailed a finger in the sand. "We're probably leaving soon."

"Yeah? That's too bad."

"I know. I wanted to get to know you better."

"You did? You always seemed to be chasing me off."

"I don't know. I guess I was shy."

I waited for him to kiss me then. I had Joe's impatient voice in my head: *Let's get this show on the road.*

But Wally just cleared his throat and looked out at the ocean. So I gave up and kissed him instead. Right on the cheek. He turned and our noses bumped. Then he planted one on me, right on the mouth.

The sand scratched my legs and I could feel it blowing against my back. We ground our mouths together until my teeth hurt. I put my hand experimentally on his leg, and I felt him shudder. We kept up the kissing until the boredom got to me and I started thinking about how his knee was grinding against mine. I wanted to tear my mouth away and scream.

But something was happening to Wally. He was breathing hard through his nose. I could smell him now, all sweat and a little bit of salt and maybe the hair tonic that kept his hair so wet. I started to wonder if Forney the manager kept a bottle of it behind the desk for himself and the bellboys, a snort of Vitalis instead of whiskey every couple of hours.

He put his hand on my chest and squeezed.

This was where I was supposed to stop him, but I didn't. I wanted to *know*.

I felt a surge of the power my mother had. I could see that Wally wasn't thinking anymore. He was heading straight for what he wanted with a determination that was out of his control, a train jumping the tracks and never losing speed.

I moved my hand to where I felt Peter that night, and Wally inhaled, and then things got a little out of my control, because it was like I was waving him on, saying *go ahead go ahead don't stop* even though that was far from what I was feeling. I wanted things to keep going slowly. I wanted to stay bored.

He pushed me back and ground against me. He fumbled down in his pants and I felt something naked against my bare leg. It felt soft and firm. It didn't feel threatening, but I was suddenly aware of Wally's weight, of his breath on my neck, too hot.

I had to grab for air with my hands. I was suffocating. My leg was pinned underneath his knee, and his chin was digging into my shoulder. He kept shoving against me like a piston and I couldn't breathe. I opened my eyes and saw a pimple right near his ear. My stomach rolled over. I smelled sweat and couldn't tell if it was him or me. I had learned enough.

I pushed him off as hard as I could, surprising him.

"What gives?" He rolled away, furious, moving to cover himself.

I had to scoot over on all fours to try to get up. He snatched at my skirt to stop me, and it ripped. I let out a cry that the wind took away.

"Aw, Evie." Wally tucked over himself, trying to zip up his pants. "I didn't mean it."

"I just want to go back."

"Don't tell anyone. I didn't mean it." Wally looked scared.

"I won't tell anyone," I said. "I just want to go back."

"Sure. Sure. I'll walk you."

I lurched in the sand, walking like a drunk. We were halfway back when I started to cry. Wally walked carefully, trying not to brush me with an arm or a hand, trying not to touch me at all, afraid of what I'd do.

I'd wanted to learn what love was like, but this wasn't what I'd felt with Peter. It was cheap and stupid and it stayed with you. It was animal and mineral, it was a bad taste and a terrible feeling.

"Look, you're a swell girl. I didn't think of you that way. Promise."

I couldn't stop crying, and I didn't know if it was him or thinking of not being with Peter or feeling sick.

"Evie, I've got to leave you here. I'd better not walk you in."

I saw through my tears that we were at the hotel. Wally was nervous and scared and apologetic all at once. He was practically on his toes, ready to run.

"It's okay."

Just then Mr. Forney came out on the steps for a smoke. He gave us a hard look, from my face to my clothes to Wally's pants.

"Wally, I need to see you," he said. "Double-time."

I ran across the parking lot, toward the side door that only the maids were supposed to use.

I hoped it would be the last time I'd ever see Wally. I hoped the hurricane would come so it could blow us all the way back to New York.

They didn't come back at three, or four. They didn't come back by cocktail time. I told Forney, who called Wally's dad and then, when Wally's dad said they weren't back, the Coast Guard. They didn't come back by dinner. As the afternoon wore on, the seas got higher, and a report came in that the hurricane was headed this way. It would not go south or north, it was coming right here.

The wind was blowing like crazy and the rain was starting when the chief of the Palm Beach police came to see me. He had kind eyes, and he looked worried even though he tried not to look worried. The fear I had inside bloomed and spread out through my body. My hands shook.

"Was there an experienced sailor in the group?" he asked.

"Yes. Peter. Peter Coleridge. They said they'd be back in two hours. Something must be wrong."

He exchanged a look with Forney and it was like a comic strip in a newspaper with a bubble over their heads saying "Dumb Tourists!"

"Don't worry, miss. The seas were probably more than they could handle and they put in somewhere. I've got the word out all the way up to Jupiter and down to Fort Lauderdale. We'll find them."

I lay on my bed, not sleeping. Maybe they'd pulled in somewhere, like the man said. Maybe the storm would veer off. Tomorrow morning I was set to evacuate. They'd be back by morning. I knew that. Because if I closed my eyes and thought of them out on that churning sea, I went crazy. Mom. Peter. Joe. On one little boat.

Chapter 24

There were only three others in the lobby before dawn the next morning. The maids had knocked on our doors, waking us up with the news that the island was being evacuated. The other guests had left the night before, Crabby Couple back to Missouri, the others getting in their cars late yesterday afternoon and going home. I'd heard car doors slamming and voices saying, "Hurry up, why don't you," up until ten o'clock last night.

The rain sounded almost friendly, pattering on the windows, but every so often a hard downpour would drown out what we were saying, and we'd all look outside at the palms thrashing around in the wind.

Forney poured tea and coffee and put out plates of doughnuts. Mean Fat Man kept bellowing to Forney that he didn't see why he had to leave the hotel, he'd seen worse storms in Detroit. Honeymoon Couple looked scared, even the husband.

"I told you we should have left yesterday," Honeymoon Wife said in a loud whisper to him. She wore a little blue hat with white flowers, which trembled every time she shook her head at him. Her ankles were crossed, just the way we were taught in Deportment.

"I talked to a fellow who said only tourists were scared of hurricanes," replied Honeymoon Husband. "Down here, they have a cocktail party and ride it out."

"And where's this friend of yours now, Norman?" she whispered. "While I have to evacuate with a bunch of crackers?"

"They'll have sandwiches there, I heard," I said, trying to be helpful.

She gave me a nasty look. Later I found out that crackers meant poor Southerners, not Uneeda Biscuits.

In the little suitcase at my feet was a jumble of things. I didn't know what to pack. I'd gone through Mom's things and Joe's things because I knew they'd want me to. I packed Mom's jewelry and Joe's favorite tie and Mom's new favorite cocktail dress and her blue high heels, everything mixed in together in my suitcase because I was living with panic in my stomach now. I threw in Mom's perfume because if she was gone I'd want to still smell her. I didn't even think that I could walk into any drugstore and buy it for three ninety-five. I needed her half-full bottle.

I rode with Mr. Forney as he led the others in their cars over the Royal Palm Bridge into West Palm Beach. I peered out through the windshield, getting a look at things with every sweep of the wipers. The sky was a greasy yellow and the lake had turned a dark gray. It was moving like a great beast, rolling and crashing against the docks. I could hear the clamor of the sailboat lines hitting the masts. It sounded like bells ringing, warning us something scary was coming.

On the radio there had been instructions for evacuees. Pack food if you have it. Bring diapers for babies and toys for children. Watch out for flying coconuts.

This was how screwball the world had become. My parents and my love were lost at sea. And coconuts were falling from the sky.

"I let Wally go yesterday," Mr. Forney said. "I just want you to know that."

"You fired him?"

"Of course. Fraternizing with hotel guests is cause for dismissal."

"But —"

"We have high standards for the hotel, Miss Spooner. That includes employees."

"Yeah," I said. "I've seen your high standards up close, Mr. Forney. I think you like rolling in your stinky high standards. Especially when you can kick a couple of guests out of the hotel because they have the wrong last name."

He didn't say another word all the way to the courthouse.

I hadn't been afraid of the hurricane. But then it hit.

I learned that even before it started, the air could be full of danger. Things flew — signs, branches, screen doors. The rain could come down so hard you couldn't hear people talking right next to you. You felt the air and the wind in your belly, like a pressure inside, and putting your hands over your ears only made it worse.

I learned that a roof could fly off a building. That's what we were all afraid of in the courthouse. We sat on the long benches, or lay down, and even the children didn't cry, just the babies. The families stayed tight together, the mothers petting their children like puppy dogs. And I was alone.

Everyone kept talking about their houses and the hurricane of '28 and the thousand people who died out in Pahokee. Wherever that was. People were saying "I remember" and "Did you check on Marylou?" and "We should have stayed with the house." Someone said the winds were over a hundred miles an hour now.

A woman with a plain, strong face brought me a blanket. "Here you go, precious. Don't you worry now. The storm will blow itself out. It always does." I'd seen her talking to a policeman, and he must have told her about me, because she brought me soup, too, so I didn't have to wait in line.

It was as dark as nighttime. The lights went out. The wind made the windows shake. The roof rattled.

They couldn't be out there in this. They would have to be somewhere on land, waiting it out. That was it: The wind and the waves had gotten bad, and somehow they couldn't get back, so they pulled in somewhere to wait it out, and there wasn't a phone, or stupid Forney was too busy closing shutters to answer the phone.

After the storm had blown through (because it was going to blow through, eventually — that had to happen, even with the biggest storm), I would walk out into the streets, and everything would be all right, and Peter would be walking down the block, looking for me, and he'd say:

I've been searching for you everywhere.

The storm would bring us together and make us realize that he would wait for me, we would be sweethearts until we could marry. I knew it was a crackpot dream, but I couldn't stop dreaming it.

I closed my eyes and dreamed that dream, and the hours passed. The wind stopped, and I lifted my head, but the man next to me said, "It's the eye, girl."

"The eye? Then it's almost over."

"It's only half over."

Half over? Some of the boys and men went outside in the yellow light and came back and someone asked how it was and they said, "Pretty bad." Trees down and the storm surge had made Clematis into a river. A building had collapsed right on the street outside.

As I curled up into a ball and tried to rock myself to comfort, a roar of a freight train passing close hit my ears. It was the wind. It started all over again.

Eventually, the storm ended. It blew out of town, sucking away buildings and trees and sending the lake spilling into the streets of West Palm.

There was nowhere to go. They weren't allowing anyone to go back to Palm Beach. The hotel was closed. I sat on the bench. The nice woman left, and someone gave me a pastry and some juice.

A man came over to me, dressed in dirty pants and a shirt. "Sorry, I've been out cleaning up this morning," he said, gesturing to his clothes. I realized he was wearing a police uniform. "We got hit pretty bad. I'm Officer Deary."

"Did you find my parents?" It was the question I didn't want to ask. Dreading the answer.

"Not yet," he said kindly. "But my wife and me, we live close by. The street isn't too bad. My Twyla's a good cook, and we got a propane stove going. So come on with me, and you can have some coffee and breakfast. We better hurry before she starts feeding the neighborhood and the food runs out."

I hesitated.

"Don't worry now — every police officer knows right where you'll be. Soon as we hear something, I'll come see you. Things are crazy everywhere, phone service dead, most places. But we'll find them."

So I took my suitcase and I followed him outside and I thought maybe, for the first time, I understood all those pictures in the paper I saw from the war. Bombs could have done this, knocked down buildings and trees, turned cars on their sides. It seemed like a dream. The world had exploded, and I was standing with a stranger, the person who would be the one, probably, to tell me that everyone I loved was dead.

Chapter 25

Twyla Deary was a thin woman in a housedress, with a skinny auburn braid that ran down her back. She had a thick Southern accent and a habit of repeating part of what she'd just said. She had set up a pot of coffee and had made plates and plates of sandwiches, and after clucking over me and saying "Don't you worry, dearie, things have a way of turning out just fine, now don't you worry now" and handing me a sandwich with her homemade marmalade and cream cheese, she ran back to the kitchen to make more food.

She put me to work, too, because "idle hands make twice the worry." I was happy to cut bread into slices and make more coffee and lemonade for the barefoot children who came shyly knocking on the frame of the open back door.

Their house had survived better than many I'd seen

("Because my Bud made sure we were snug and tight, he went through the 1928 hurricane when he was a boy, so Bud is the only living soul who's prepared for Armageddon. Prepared for Armageddon, I tell you"), but there was a river running outside the front door. I'd had to take off my shoes to wade to the porch with Officer Deary.

I had a marmalade sandwich on a flowered plate for comfort, and people I didn't know coming in and out the door saying "Now, how did you fare, Twyla?" while they couldn't wait to tell their own hurricane stories. Then came the whispers about "that poor child, parents lost at sea, maybe," and finally I had to double over, grab fistfuls of my skirt in my hands and do what I'd forgotten to do during the whole last night: pray.

A few hours later, Sheriff Bud Deary waded through the water and arrived, grimy and wet and exhausted, to tell me my parents had been found. Joe and Bev had been blown off-course, had brought the boat into the mangroves near Munyon Island, wherever that was, and left the boat in a hurricane hole. They'd gotten ashore by wading and swimming, tying themselves together with rope. They couldn't make it back, so they broke into a restaurant and rode out the storm there.

"A hurricane hole?" I shook my head, remembering the night Peter had mentioned it.

You and me should find ourselves a hurricane hole.

"Your parents stumbled on it, I guess. They were lucky to get to shore."

They were alive. Alive. Mom. I felt her invade me, and I let her in. I started laughing and crying, the relief was so real. I felt Twyla patting me on the back, saying *there, there* over and over.

And then I stopped on a dime. There was something wrong. Something I wasn't hearing.

I was so breathless I could only get out one word. "Peter?"

"A family friend, I understand." The way his voice went so gentle then — I knew.

"He went overboard when they were in the ocean. The engine died, he was trying to fix it below, in the engine well. There was a rogue wave. According to your parents, he got hit in the head by something — a wrench, they think — and he came up topside. He seemed okay, but he must have been dizzy, because he went over. They said it happened so quick. One minute he was there, they could see him, and the next minute a swell came — the wind was gusting about that time, maybe forty miles per hour — and he got knocked off his feet. They tried to get him in the boat, your mother took the helm, your dad threw him all the life preservers, but they saw him go down."

"But he's a good swimmer," I said.

"Jesus is merciful," Twyla said. "Jesus is merciful, child. Your parents are safe."

"He's not dead, no matter what you think," I said. "He grew up around the water. Maybe he swam to shore, maybe he'll turn up, just the way they did. Things are crazy everywhere, you said."

The sheriff exchanged a glance with his Twyla.

"Your parents are trying to get up here to you," he said. "The Clearview Hotel here in West Palm is open. They'll take you in. Your parents will be here by afternoon. Police escort."

"He could have swum to shore!" I shouted. Because if I could get him to say it, it would be true.

"Twyla, honey, pack her a couple of sandwiches," he said instead.

"I'll do that right now. Don't you worry, ladybug," Twyla said, patting my shoulder. "Don't you worry now."

Ladybug and pussycat, nicknames to call a girl you pity.

Did he pity me?

Peter, please come back so you can tell me. Tell me if you love me.

I'll die if I don't know if you love me.

You swam to shore. It was hard but you did it because you're so strong. You walked and walked until you found shelter. Now you're trying to get back here.

I will be Twyla Deary. I will say everything twice until you come back to me. I will find the thing to do that will bring you back.

Live.

Live.

Chapter 26

They got to me late that afternoon. Mom's white and pink sundress was filthy. She was barefoot. Joe looked worse. His pants looked like he'd used them for a mop in a fish store. His shirt was missing a button or two, open at his throat. I could see how thick his throat was, the black hair curling up in a snaky line. The policeman who had brought them stood back a couple of paces while they hurried to me outside the hotel's front door.

Mom put her arms around me. "Baby, I thought I'd never see you again." I smelled water standing in a drain, and something else, sharp, like ammonia.

I stepped back before she was ready, maybe. Joe leaned over and kissed me. "You're a sight for sore eyes."

"What about Peter? What happened?" I could feel the policeman's eyes on me, and I wondered why he didn't go.

"It was a terrible storm," Joe said.

"We almost drowned," Mom said. "I need a bath." She said it in a way that was almost angry, like we were standing in her way. She wasn't herself. I knew that, I could see that she hardly knew where she was, or if she was standing up straight.

"I'll let you folks get settled," the policeman said. "If there's any word, I'll come by."

"Thank you, officer," Joe said in his best-manners voice.

As we walked through the lobby, my mother pressed close to me.

"It was like an awful dream," she said. "Like it wasn't happening to me at all."

"We made it to shelter, but I thought the building would blow out to sea any minute," Joe said. "I'll tell you one thing: I'm through with Florida."

I showed them our room. No more suite for us. We had two double beds and a couch, the furniture all crowded together. It was dark. They hadn't taken off the shutters over the windows yet. I switched on the light.

"Glad this place has electricity," Joe said.

"It was so dark where we were," Mom said.

She saw the open suitcase on the bed and started to go through it. She shook out her blue cocktail dress. "This is the only thing you brought for me? Honestly! How do you expect me to wear this in broad daylight!"

"I didn't know what to bring," I said. "I didn't think."

"I'll go back to the Mirage," Joe said. "I'll get your clothes, Bev."

"No!" Mom's voice was sharp and on the edge of something. "Don't make waves, Joe."

It was a funny choice of words, but none of us laughed.

"He wasn't what you thought," Mom whispered to me that night. We lay together in one of the double beds. Joe snored in the other one. "He wasn't what I thought, either. Joe set me straight. I should have known what he was, the way he went after you that way."

I was curled up, facing the wall. She was behind me, her voice thick and urgent.

"He followed us down here, you know. He was black-mailing Joe. He was holding something over his head. Peter thought Joe owed him money. They had some deal, and Peter thought one thing and Joe thought another. That's all. And so Peter said he'd go to the Graysons and tell them Joe was a welsher, that he'd walk away from a debt. You and I know that isn't true. The thing is, though, this came at a really bad time for Joe. You know he just opened up two more businesses. He put all of our cash into them. So he was trapped. That's why Peter made up to us and took us places. He flattered us and we liked his company because of that. Peter went after you behind my — behind *our* backs. He was using you, too. Evie? Are you listening?"

No, it wasn't like that. It wasn't like that at all.

But it *looked* like that.

I wanted to put the pillow over my ears. I wished she'd just shut up. So much noise was in my head.

"I'm just lucky I showed up that night at his house. Who knows what could have happened? Nothing happened before that, right, baby?"

I didn't answer her.

"Because if it did, it's all right. You shouldn't feel . . . he was trying to get at Joe any way he could. Nothing was your fault. Nothing, baby. I had to tell Joe what happened. He doesn't blame you. Not in the least. But the thing is . . . we probably shouldn't tell anyone about any of this. Better to just keep our mouths shut, since Peter's missing. Joe wants to head back to New York. We're going to go back just as soon as we can. Won't you like that? Don't you miss your friends?"

No, I didn't miss my friends.

"We don't belong here."

No, we didn't belong here.

"If we can just get home, everything will be all right."

She said this like it was true.

"We can be just like we were. I promise, Evie. You're the most important thing in the world to me," she whispered.

"Mom." I gulped in air so I could get the question out. "What really happened? Tell me. What happened on the boat?"

She rolled away from me. "Just what we said, baby. Now go to sleep."

I walked through the fallen trees and branches to the bridge over to the island. The lake was still cloudy and thick from the storm but the sun was out. The sky was blue again. Just a few blocks from me, you couldn't walk along the path beside the lake, the water was so deep. They said you could take a rowboat down the main street in Delray Beach. The tiki huts were gone and so was the boardwalk. The roof had been blown off the casino in Lake Worth.

We'll be back! He'd yelled it at me, waving as the boat took off.

Think of all the people in the world who said *Be back soon!* and didn't come back. That's what we found out during the war.

People kept saying about the hurricane, *At least it's not as bad as '28.* Because no matter how bad something is, there's always something worse to compare it to. Some people find that comforting for some reason.

I didn't.

Joe wanted to leave, but he couldn't get to his car. There was no gas, anyway. You could only buy a buck at most, not enough to get you very far. We were stuck.

"I'm guessing you wouldn't want to leave yet, anyway," Officer Deary said when he dropped by the next day. "Not with your friend still missing."

We kept the radio on all the time. My head was full of music. The songs told me what would happen. I'd be seeing him in all the old familiar places. I wouldn't want to walk without him. These foolish things reminded me of him. Won't you tell him please to put on some speed. My dream would be here beside me.

He would come back. He would tell me the truth behind the lies. We would fill up his blue convertible with gas and we would take off, the way we had on those other long, hot afternoons, when there was nobody in the world but us.

The hotel sent our suitcases over. Joe got a ride over to pick up his car. He said it seemed like hundreds of palm trees were blown down. Green coconuts were lying smashed on the streets.

The roads weren't bad north of us. And he had found a place to sell him a tank full of gas. We were leaving tomorrow. After a good night's sleep and with a thermos full of coffee, because he'd drive all day and all night if he had to, as far as he could, just to get home.

Mom kept the lamp on the vanity burning all night long. I lay on my side and watched the shaft of light on the floor. I listened to her turn over in bed. I fell asleep to the sound of restless legs and whispering sheets. The sounds merged together in my head, in my dreams, and I wasn't sure if I'd heard Joe and Mom whispering together or if I'd been dreaming.

We were packing the car before sunup when the cruiser pulled up. Officer Deary got out. "Taking off?"

We all stopped what we were doing, Mom with a suitcase ready to slide in the trunk, me carrying a stack of magazines. Joe put his hand on my shoulder. "I like to get an early start."

"Well, I'm afraid I'm going to have to ask you to stay for a few more days," the sheriff said.

"Officer Deary, we've been here for two days since the hurricane," Joe said. "You have my address in New York. I have several businesses to run. This delay is costing me."

Officer Deary nodded a few times. "I appreciate that, I surely do. I know how busy you Northerners are. Peter Coleridge's body has been found."

I gasped. The sentence had come without warning. There was no *I came here to tell you* or *I have news.*

It was the word *body.* I could see it, something heavy, like a log, not like a person, turning with the waves, bumping up on a beach.

Mom dropped the suitcase. Pebbles shifted, a fallen palm leaf blew, the fronds *tap-tap-tapping* against the trunk of the tree.

"We'd like to ask you and your wife some questions," Officer Deary said. "Right now."

Chapter 27

They left, and I was left with this, that Peter was dead.

I couldn't cry.

You have to have your arms open and your mouth open and your heart. My heart was a fist.

Maybe it wasn't him that they found, maybe it was someone else. Someone not as lucky as Peter, not as golden, not as charmed.

Could I go back, why couldn't I go back, why couldn't I stop them from taking out the boat, why couldn't I go back and stop Peter from going?

I'd given Mr. Grayson's letter to Joe. Joe knew he could still make a deal. He thought Peter stood in his way.

If I thought back to what might have happened on that boat, my brain just locked.

Joe that morning, so jovial and false. And Peter so

wary. And Mom so stunned and numb, like she couldn't resist Joe.

The three of them on that boat.

And Peter's strange smile.

Let me put it this way: I think he'd be a hell of lot happier if I disappeared.

"There are some things we have to talk about," Mom said when they got back. She'd gone right for a cigarette, and Joe had gone right for a drink. "Things we need to get straight between us. Because the police might want to talk to you, and we should make sure you remember how things really happened. They separated me and Joe, in little rooms, tried to trip us up on things. Detectives questioned us, not that nice Officer Deary."

"But we were ahead of them, weren't we, baby doll?" Joe asked. He looked rattled, though, no matter what he said.

"What things?" I asked.

"How we met Peter, what we did with him, things like that," Mom said. She was talking to me but her eyes kept flitting to Joe, like a sparrow darting back and forth between the lawn and a branch. "That we were friends, holiday friends, like that. We didn't know him terribly well."

"But everyone saw us," I said. "We saw him every day."

"Well, sure," Joe said. "But casual-like. The way you strike up a friendship on vacation with someone you barely knew before."

"And he really wanted to go out on the boat that day, so we said all right," Mom said.

"But Joe said —"

"No, it was Peter," Joe said. "You remember, Bev. He was talking about how good he was at handling a boat, am I right?"

"I remember," Mom said. "Don't you remember, Evie?"

I didn't say anything.

"Evie, the thing is," Mom said, "the police here? They don't like New Yorkers."

"This one cop, he kept asking me if I was a Jew," Joe said. "Because they heard the story about the Graysons, I figure. Can you beat that? I was an altar boy. Not that I'd tell him I was Catholic. They don't like Catholics, either."

"So, if you don't remember something clearly, like who said what, then maybe it's better to say you don't remember at all," Mom said. "Understand?"

I did understand. "You want me to lie," I said.

"Do you get it?" Joe's face was dark. "They're trying to pin this on me!"

"Joe." Mom's voice sharpened. "No sense scaring Evie."

"Why not? I'm plenty scared!" Joe took a pull on his drink. When he turned back to me, his voice was softer.

"Say, kiddo. A lot of things have happened. We just lived through a hurricane, right? And we're just saying that things can get hazy. And cops can twist things, and the next thing you know, they've trumped up a case where there is no case, just to get themselves in the headlines. They do the third degree down here. They know how to beat a man without marking him."

"Joe!"

"She should know what could happen!"

I thought of the cops, and the third degree, and a soft voice asking me questions, and me having to think before I answered, me having to be careful. Then I thought of why they were telling me this, and that made me more scared.

Joe gripped my arms hard. "We're a family. What's that thing you and your mom say? We stick together like glue. Right?" He waited for my nod. "That's my girl."

Over his shoulder, I looked into Mom's eyes. I didn't see someone I recognized. I saw someone smaller. Someone scared. Scared of the police? Scared of Joe?

No. My mother was scared of me.

Chapter 28

DROWNING OF NEW YORK TOURIST
DEEMED SUSPICIOUS
Couple Questioned in Mysterious Death
Coroner Expected to Call for Inquest

walked all the way downtown to buy the paper. I
didn't want to buy it at the newsstand in the lobby.
I read it at the deserted bandshell, surrounded by
men cleaning up the fallen branches. My blouse was
soaked, I'd gotten so hot on the walk, but I shivered as
I read.

> *Peter Coleridge, twenty-three, a wealthy tourist*
> *from Oyster Bay, Long Island, fell overboard on the*
> *afternoon of September seventeenth, the day before*
> *landfall of the hurricane. Winds were gusting up to*
> *fifty knots and there were numerous squalls out on the*

ocean. Coleridge, Mr. Joseph Spooner, and his wife, Beverly Spooner, from Brooklyn, New York, hired a boat, the Captive Lady, from Captain Stephen "Sandy" Forrest at the town dock on Wednesday.

According to the police, the engine of the Captive Lady failed during high seas while the group motored from the Palm Beach inlet toward Jupiter. Mr. Coleridge made an attempt to repair the engine, placing a wrench on the deck above while he worked below in the engine well. The motion of the boat sent the wrench into the engine well, striking him on the head. Stunned from the blow, he came up on deck, and a rogue wave sent him overboard.

Mr. and Mrs. Spooner attempted to rescue him, to no avail.

Mr. Coleridge's body washed up near Manalapan, where a surf caster, Kelly Marin, discovered it early Thursday morning.

Beverly Spooner, an attractive blonde, and Joseph Spooner, a businessman, were guests of Le Mirage on Palm Beach island, along with the deceased.

The coroner's report included "suspicious markings" that could be "inconsistent" with the "natural batterings" that a body would be prone to sustain during such a hurricane.

Mr. Coleridge's father, Ellis Coleridge, a fisherman,

has journeyed from his home in Patchogue, Long Island, to identify his son's body. He was unavailable for comment.

A fisherman?

It was all in next day's morning edition. Peter wasn't loaded. They found that out pretty fast. He'd never been to college, let alone Yale. He was an only child. All through high school he'd worked summers at a country club in Oyster Bay. That's where he'd borrowed his manners from. And the blue convertible. The friend he'd borrowed it from had reported it stolen when Peter had taken it and hadn't returned.

Everything he'd told me about himself had been a lie.

The family friend with the house in Palm Beach? Just a mansion, closed until the season. He'd broken in. A caretaker had found evidence that someone was staying there when he'd gone over to check before the hurricane. A window had been forced. There were glasses left on a sill. Two of them. One of them had lipstick traces. Dark red, the paper said.

The most tempting color since Eve winked at Adam.

By the afternoon edition, the mansion was called a "secret love nest." And Beverly had gone from "attractive blonde" to a suspect.

Peter wasn't who I thought he was. Could it be that Mom wasn't, either?

If everyone was wondering what had gone on between Peter and my mother, wouldn't I be crazy not to wonder, too?

SUSPICIONS GROW ON
COLERIDGE DROWNING
Mystery Woman Sought
Inquest to Begin on Friday
Judge Alton Friend to Preside

Joe Spooner, the man I'd picked to be my dad.

This man who bent over to turn the key of a neighbor kid's roller skate — could he have killed somebody? This man who knew how to tie a bow on the sash of my party dress, who took me for egg creams in Manhattan drugstores for the adventure of it? This man who'd say, after I'd had a fight with Margie, "Aw, kid, you gotta let bygones be bygones. Here's a dime, go buy yourselves a couple of Cokes."

This man couldn't be a killer.

Killers were in movies.

Killers didn't snore in the bed next to you.

And Mom. Whatever had happened to her with

Peter — which I couldn't, wouldn't think about — she was still my mother. She'd still tucked me in at night, she'd still washed my blouses out in the sink every night even in winter with red cold hands, she'd still groaned every morning when the alarm went off and got up anyway and made my Ovaltine and toast. She was the one who cried hardest when the puppy she gave me for Christmas died of distemper. I remembered that puppy in her lap, his mouth all foam, while she cried a bucket of tears.

She couldn't have been part of it, if it was the thing I kept seeing when I closed my eyes: Joe hitting Peter on the head, Joe pushing Peter into the churning ocean.

Imagine our surprise when we got back from lunch the next day and found Grandma Glad in our room. She still had her going-out hat on, a dark green hat with stiff speckled feathers on one side. Her brown suitcase was on my bed. She sat on the couch, her eyes on the door. Her feet were planted on either side of an old tan leather valise that had belonged to her husband, Joe. "Big Joe Spooner," they used to call him. He died when Joe was eighteen, a big shot who'd left them in debt.

"When were you going to tell me, Joe?" she asked.

"How did you get here?" Joe looked genuinely stunned.

"Eastern Airlines flight to Miami, then I hired a car. When were you going to tell me?"

"You flew in a plane?" This was maybe more shocking than her sudden appearance.

"It made the papers in New York. I read about it in the *paper*. I left messages here, but you never called me back."

"You took a plane?"

"I read it in the newspaper, Joe!"

"I didn't want to worry you, Ma."

"So I can be half-killed, reading it in the paper. I almost fainted dead on the floor, and me alone in the house." Grandma Glad eyed Mom like she was a week-old fish. "You need better help than you've got."

"We didn't do anything wrong," Joe said.

"You're crazy if you don't see that it doesn't matter," Grandma Glad said. "They want to pin it on you. Can't you read the papers? And you don't help matters. What are you talking to a reporter for?"

"He called me. He asked a question."

"I talked to John Reilly," Grandma Glad said. John Reilly was a fat lawyer with a red face. Everybody went to him for wills and deeds and when their kid got caught doing something.

"That shyster," Mom muttered.

"That shyster knows his business. He says don't talk to reporters — you put your foot in it and you can't get it out. You said in the paper you didn't understand why they called the inquest. Dumb, Mr. Reilly said. He said, you say you *welcome* the inquest."

Joe dropped his head in his hands. "What am I going to do?"

"What's the most important thing down here?"

I couldn't get over it. There Gladys sat, in her navy flowered dress, her Red Cross shoes planted firmly on the carpet. She had gotten some authority somehow, and it wasn't just because she'd talked to a lawyer. Gladys Spooner, sitting in a chair, listening to the radio, looking out the window, gossiping on the porch. All that time, she was gathering information for just this moment to take over.

"The tourists," Grandma Glad went on. "Murder hits the papers and they have to take care of it so the tourists keep coming."

Mom went pale. "It's not a *murder*. Nobody's calling it a murder."

"They are, and we might as well, too, or else, how are we going to fight?" Grandma Glad said. I hated her for using the word out loud, but she made us all shut up, that's for sure. Once the word was out, we had to face it square. I hated her for it, but she was right.

"I'm sunk," Joe said. "I'm a nobody. They'll pin it on me, all right."

"You're not a nobody," Grandma Glad said fiercely. "*He* was a nobody."

I started to cry, but nobody paid attention, even when I had to put my hands over my mouth so that the noise wouldn't go out into the hall. Peter was there in the room with me suddenly. I could see the golden hair on his forearms, the way he twisted his mouth when he was trying not to smile at me. A *nobody*. He was still so clear and so alive and so much him. There was so much *Peter* inside me I felt sick.

Dead. My stomach twisted as it hit me again. Dead.

"I told you not to marry her," Grandma Glad said. It was like me and Mom weren't even in the room. "I told you she was trouble. I said she'd run around on you."

"Yeah, and you kept on saying it, even when Joe was overseas and I was working to put food on your table!" Mom said.

"Working." Grandma Glad sniffed. "Is that what you call it? Is that what you were doing with that Coldidge fellow?"

"Coleridge," I said. My voice was all choked and wavery. "His name was Coleridge." I couldn't stand hearing her. I had pushed evil away, I had tried to keep everything straight, and even though everything was horrible, she'd walked in the door and brought evil in.

"This isn't helping any," Joe said. "We can't fight each other. Not now."

"I'm going to get you out of this, Joey," Grandma Glad said.

"What about me?" Mom asked, her voice quiet. "You going to leave me in the soup, Gladys? You going to pin it on me and let your boy go free? This is Christmas for you, isn't it? Wrap me up and hand me over with a big fat bow."

That stopped my crying. Mom had put her finger on it, all right. That was the possibility in the room, and I wasn't even seeing it.

Grandma Glad hesitated. She let Mom swing on the rope for a while.

"Ma?" Joe said.

You could tell she was about to eat some week-old brussels sprouts because they were the only things in the icebox. She didn't want the taste of what she was about to say in her mouth. "What happens to you, happens to my boy," she said to Mom. "I'd let you stew in the soup if I could. But I can't."

"I'm crazy about you, too, Gladys," Mom said, and she blew out cigarette smoke right in her face.

I gave up my bed that night to Grandma Glad and bunked on the couch. Joe pushed it closer to the bed so

Grandma Glad could get out to the toilet on the other side in the middle of the night if she had to.

The couch smelled like cigarettes and mildew. It was small, and I had to stick my legs up on the arm or curl up in a ball to be comfortable, which I wasn't.

I woke up to whispers in the middle of the night. For a second I didn't know where I was. I stared at the blinds for a minute, trying to remember. All I saw were clouds glowing, like the moon was trying to bust out from behind.

Grandma Glad sat on the edge of the bed, Joe right next to her. I could have touched her red slipper, touched her big toe with its thick yellow nail. If I wanted to.

It's funny how adults are. When they think a kid is asleep, they never expect you to wake up and listen.

"You don't ever let them know that you knew about her and him," Grandma Glad said. "If it comes out, you didn't know."

"She says it's all lies. She says he chased her, but she put him off. She liked the attention, she said. I was busy with the Grayson fellow, trying to swing a deal. Is that a crime? It was Evie he went after, she said."

"You never were a chump, Joe. Don't start now. How do you think she got along all those years?"

I wanted to leap up and scream at her that it wasn't true. I knew that. I knew Mom. All she had was her reputation. She wouldn't give them the satisfaction of having gossip about her, she said. That's why she dragged me to church every Sunday and nodded and smiled to the ladies as we walked up in our hats and white gloves.

I had been thinking of the wives of the men who whistled as Beverly Plunkett went by, of them being the gossips. That wasn't the enemy for Mom. All the time, her enemy had been waiting. Her enemy was sitting in the green chair in the living room.

"She says I neglected her."

"You were building your business. Nobody did as good as you after the war."

"I haven't been a saint, Ma. When I was overseas —"

"You were a soldier. A hero. You made your way, best you could. Now stop it, Joey. We've got to get this straight, now. Reilly says to hire a lawyer. He gave me a name. Things aren't always on the up-and-up, you know. If we know the right people, maybe we can close this down. That's what he says — without coming right out and saying it, mind you. If you spread the green, he said, certain people will look the other way. I came down with eight thousand."

"Ma!" Joe's voice burst out, and she shushed him.

"We'll only use it if we have to."

"That's all the money I've got in the world. It's going to buy us a dream house."

211

So Joe had cash, all this time. He could have paid Peter, and he didn't. He wanted his dream house instead. He wouldn't give that up. But Grandma Glad knew about the money.

So many lies around me. Enough lies to fill ten houses.

"Forget the house — this is your life. You saw your chance in the war, you took it, you made something of yourself. Just like your dad."

"Pop died broke."

"Hush your mouth, the man did his best. You'll make it through this. We'll try for the police chief. A bribe here and there. Maybe the judge. Reilly says to ask our lawyer when we get one, and he'll give us the straight deal. But don't ask until we have to."

The shadows moved apart. Joe went back to his bed. Grandma Glad took off her robe and got back into her bed. I kept my eyes almost closed. I watched her pull the covers up to her chin.

I didn't understand. There was so much I didn't get.

But one thing shone through, like the moon through the clouds, silver now painting my blanket.

She told him this and that and what they were going to do and how bad my mother was.

But never once did she ask him if he did it.

Chapter 29

Headlines. Words that once you read upside down, that popped out at you at a newsstand as you roller-skated by, or from the kitchen table as you went by to grab an apple from a yellow bowl on the kitchen counter. BODY and BLONDE and MURDER.

Now they were about us.

Grandma Glad went into action. It was like she'd been drafted and had blown through basic in a week. She started telling Joe what to do. The first thing she did, she hired a lawyer. She said we needed a local guy on our side. This guy, Mr. Markel, was a tall, pale man with a stretched-out face and rimless glasses covering colorless eyes. I couldn't exactly see him facing down the enemy. The most he did, from what I could see, was tell Joe and Mom what to wear at the inquest. When Mom told him that she didn't have any navy or gray outfits, he'd said, "Buy some."

They wouldn't let me go to the inquest the first day. Mom wore a gray dress with a white collar and a black straw hat. Joe wore a suit and tie. Grandma Glad wore her diamond pin.

"The good news is that the coroner's report says Coleridge did die by drowning," Markel said. He'd stopped over for coffee before the inquest.

I saw Mom swallow. "Why is that good news?"

"Because if he'd died from a blow to the head, for example, they would have had more of a case that he was dead when he hit the water."

Mom turned her face away. "You certainly don't mince words, do you."

He looked over at her. "No."

They were gone almost all day. I went downtown for the afternoon edition. I took it to the bandshell and held it in my lap for a minute. The park had been cleaned up and the branches carted away. The lake was gray, stealing color from the sky.

I could see the headline, and I didn't want to read the story.

STARTLING TESTIMONY IN COLERIDGE INQUEST

Suspicion Cast on Businessman's Wife
Surprise Witness Identifies Her in Court

214

I read it fast, trying to just make sense of the jumping words.

The witness was Iris Wright, owner of Iris's Eye, a gift shop on South Dixie Highway. A couple had come in, in high spirits, said Iris, and browsed. She remembered them because they were both "so attractive." The woman was dressed all in white. They bought a pineapple vase. They laughed together as the man paid for it. She recognized the man in the picture in the paper. And then the state's attorney, Raymond Toomer, asked her if the woman was in the courtroom.

> Mrs. Wright pointed with her chin. "That's her there."
>
> "Please rise, Mrs. Spooner," Mr. Toomer requested.
>
> Mrs. Spooner stood slowly. She was dressed in a gray silk frock with a white collar and cuffs, her bright hair obscured by a black straw hat with a pink ribbon. Mr. Toomer asked her to remove her hat. Mrs. Spooner's fingers fumbled as she did so. When she pulled it off, her blond hair tumbled to her shoulders and glinted in the sunlight that streamed through the courtroom window.
>
> Mrs. Wright positively identified Mrs. Spooner. "That's her," she said, and pointed a finger. "She's a looker. I'd recognize her anywhere."

She'd come back to the hotel with the pineapple vase the day we'd all gone to the movies. Peter had said goodbye and she'd walked off, her scarf trailing behind her. She was going to see if the shops on Worth Avenue were open, she said.

So Peter had followed her in his car. He'd probably leaned out, his elbow on the door, and said, *There's nothing open on the island. Let me take you shopping.*

I'd thought that day was my first date with Peter. It wasn't. It was Mom's.

All that time it had been him and her, not him and me.

The world went white for just an instant. Then pain roared in. With all the lies around me, this was the worst. This was the one I couldn't stomach.

I had to sit down. I had to think. I had to breathe.

When I'd heard Joe and Grandma Glad talking about it, I'd been ready to agree with Joe, to say it was just flirtation, that I was the one Peter had wanted.

But now I wasn't so blind. Not anymore. It had been between them from the very first.

What makes you think you know what ails me?

I can only guess.

Two blond heads together in a dark movie theater, close together, whispering.

Flirting. They'd been flirting the whole time, only I hadn't seen it.

Mom, running down the beach. Peter, picking her up, swinging her around. Her hands on his chest like she already knew how it felt.

She already knew how it felt.

Mom, riding in Peter's car, her lips curving in a soft smile as he drove. A secret smile, a cat over a dish of cream.

Peter putting his finger on her lips to stop her words. Letting his finger linger there longer than it should.

All that time, I'd thought Mom was in the way. I'd been the one in the way. I'd been their cover.

The knowing was so huge I couldn't bear it. I sprang off the bench and ran toward the water, ran as fast as I'd ever run in my life, ran until my lungs burned. But I couldn't run away from it. The facts slapping down like cards on a table.

The orange petals on the car. Mom had tipped Wally every day to wash them off.

She'd known how to find me at Peter's because she went there every day. She went there to be with him. And when I'd first walked up to him that night, he'd thought it was her. I was wearing her perfume, I was wearing heels.

They'd been ... something together. Something I

didn't want to know about. I thought of Peter's kiss, thought of how he must have kissed her that way.

More than that. It was sex. That was what had been between them.

I stared at the gray water. It hurt so much I could barely breathe.

The newspaper was still bunched in my hand. I smoothed it out and sat on the grass to read it.

Mr. Markel got to ask the woman from the store a few questions. He asked if she knew for sure they were a couple. Did they hold hands? Did they kiss? Iris said no, but she could tell they were in love because of the way they were smiling. Judge Friend said her opinion on smiles wasn't testimony.

Smiles. I'd seen their smiles, too. But I was a little slower on the uptake than Iris Wright.

My eyes stung with the sudden rush of wanting him. I needed Peter here to explain. The funny thing was, I still thought he'd tell me the truth. Had he loved Mom, really loved her?

Checking up on me? How considerate.

He'd been angry at her that night. Did that mean he'd regretted what they'd done? Was that why he'd turned to me that night instead of her?

I felt dizzy and sick. I couldn't bear it if I'd meant nothing to Peter. I couldn't bear being a sap.

The surf caster who found Peter testified. I skipped that part. I didn't think I could get through this if I had to think about it. I had to close it like a book, the image of him dead. I had to think of him alive. I had to think of this as happening to someone else.

The policeman who had driven Mom and Joe back to me at the hotel was next. The officer testified that for two people who had seen a man drown, they seemed more concerned about what they'd been through themselves. *I smelled liquor on them*, he said.

The state's attorney asked him what Mom had said when she saw me and realized I was okay.

"She said she needed a bath," the officer replied.

A gasp went up in the courtroom. Those sitting in back stood on their chairs to get a glimpse of Mrs. Spooner.

He made it sound like she didn't care. But she had been relieved. I knew her best, and I knew that. I knew she was dirty and scared from what she'd been through. But I knew that when we saw each other, something frantic in her lifted. Because that's the way she was. If she was upset about something, first she got mad at the mashed potatoes.

The final witness was Officer Deary.

He testified that Joe was packing the car when he drove up to tell him that the body had been found.

"Did he seem concerned about the confirmation of the death?" Mr. Toomer asked.

"I can't say for sure," the tall, plain-spoken officer replied. "He was worried about his business up in New York, he said." The courtroom stirred, and all eyes rested on Joseph Spooner, who leaned over to whisper to his attorney. Beverly Spooner gripped her mother-in-law's hand.

I blew out a breath. Now I knew the paper was bunk. First Joe and Mom were from Brooklyn, and now Mom was holding hands with Gladys. She'd sooner hold hands with a black widow spider.

Among the witnesses at tomorrow's hearing would be Joseph Spooner and Beverly Spooner.

I dug the heels of my palms into my eyes and doubled over. I could smell the newspaper, inky and damp. There were facts I was reading, and then those facts were twisted so hard they boomeranged in the wrong direction. What was the truth?

I knew that Mom and Peter had been together. But what did it mean?

If everyone else believed that Joe and Mom had killed

Peter, would I be able to hold on to believing that they didn't, even with my eyes wide open?

Later that day Joe drove me to Mr. Markel's office. I could barely look at him, and if Mom had been there, I probably would have had to jump out of the car. As soon as we got to the office, I put my hand on the door handle to get out. The clouds were low and the sky was completely black. I knew we had about two seconds to get inside before the rain started.

"Hold on a sec, Evie. Before we go up, I want to talk to you."

In the time it took for Joe to start talking, the sky opened up and dumped the rain. We had to roll up the windows. Within minutes the windows steamed up and we couldn't see outside.

Joe looked ahead, his hands quiet on the steering wheel. "So maybe I didn't get a chance to be much of a dad for you. I married your mother, I went right off into the service. I got back, I started my business. But I tried. And not just because I wanted to make your mother happy, either. I tried because you're a good kid and I want to be your dad."

"I know you tried, Joe." Was *tried* a good word when it came to loving someone?

"I miss you calling me Dad. You haven't been, lately."

Joe waited a moment or two. "Okay, okay. The thing is, the lawyer is going to talk to you about Peter, and even though he's our lawyer, I just want you to know this . . . you don't have to tell him everything. He's going to say, 'You can tell me everything, Evie,' but you don't have to. Some things are private. You had your first love with Peter, am I right? Nobody has to know about that but you. You can keep it close. You look right in his eyes when you answer. Don't smile, don't look away. The thing is, Evie . . ." Joe cleared his throat, stretched his fingers out, then grabbed the wheel again. "It's better they don't think that I knew about Peter chasing Mom. That I wondered. Like, that day at the golf course — they shouldn't know she said she was taking lessons when she wasn't. She just needed to get off by herself sometimes, she said. You see, the less we're tied to this guy, the better. Because if they start digging for stuff, they are going to find out things that wouldn't be good for the family."

"Things like what?"

"Just things."

I jerked my head and stared out the side window, even though I couldn't see anything. It was like seeing through tears in your eyes.

"Maybe I'm not your hero anymore. I can see that. Evie, look at me. Please."

I looked at him, like he asked. He looked me right in the eye.

"I didn't kill him."

"Okay."

"What I had to do during the hard times, and then during the war — that was different. I had to make my own breaks, and I did. But I didn't just do it for me."

The rain stopped. I could just make out a girl walking down the street. She had her shoes in her hands and she was walking barefoot. She walked right through a puddle, laughing. She was part of something that was so far away from me now.

"Do you remember right after I got back?" Joe asked. "We went to the city and saw a show and had dinner and came home and fell asleep, the three of us, on the couch, because we didn't want to go to bed?"

I remembered. I had felt part of them, of their love.

"That's the way it can be again. If we all stick together here. Okay? If we can just be smart now. If we can stick."

Chapter 30

The door was lettered WILSON MARKEL ATTORNEY AT LAW on the frosted glass. Joe knocked on the door and opened it.

An older woman sat at a desk right inside. There were a couple of wooden chairs and an old carpet on the floor. Not much for someone who, according to Gladys, was supposed to be the best criminal attorney in South Florida.

The woman stood. She had tight curls clustered on her forehead and the rest of her iron-gray hair tied tight back in a bun with long pins to anchor it there. It looked painful, that bun.

"How do, Miss Geiger," Joe said. "Lovely dress. This is my daughter, Evelyn Spooner."

She gave a short nod. Her gaze was like ice on a February pond. "Mr. Markel is expecting you."

She turned and walked across the floor on surprisingly high heels. If a man saw her from behind, he might follow those hips down the street. She knocked on an inner door and then opened it slightly. "Mr. Markel, the girl is here."

"Send her in, Miss Geiger."

"You may go in, Miss Spooner."

Joe started in with me, but Miss Geiger took one step toward us. "Just Miss Spooner, Mr. Spooner."

"But —"

"Just Miss Spooner. Thank you, Mr. Spooner."

I walked in. Mr. Markel was standing at his desk. He gave me the kind of smile you get from people who have a hard time smiling. It didn't help my nerves.

"Do you need me to take notes, Mr. Markel?" Miss Geiger asked.

"No, that will be all, Miss Geiger. Please shut the door."

The door closed with a soft click. I let out a long breath. "She looks at Joe like she wants to lock him up," I said.

"Miss Geiger reserves her judgment on guilt or innocence."

I didn't think so. Miss Geiger had the eyes of a judge and jury rolled into one.

"Please sit down, Miss Spooner. As your father no doubt told you, tomorrow I would like you to attend the inquest. An image of family solidarity can be a good thing. This will open you up to attention, however. You must be prepared for photographers and the press."

"All right."

"Now. Tell me about Peter Coleridge."

The words were already in my mouth, and I found them so easy to say, answering his soft questions while he watched me across the desk.

We didn't know him that well. He was another guest. He said he was from New York, too. Yes, we went out together sometimes. He said he'd teach me how to drive. No, my mother didn't see him alone. I don't remember who said to go for the boat ride even though the storm was coming. It could have been Peter.

Silence. Joe had told me not to look away, so I didn't look away.

Mr. Markel's eyes weren't colorless, they turned out to be the softest blue, the blue of a baby blanket. His silver hair was brushed straight back but little tufts made a break for it and waved around his ears.

"Was Peter Coleridge your mother's boyfriend?" His voice had been mild before, but now it whipped through the air like a slap coming out of nowhere.

"No."

"You are aware, Miss Spooner, that whatever you tell me, I can't tell to anyone, even the judge. An inquest is not a trial, but if they call you — and they might — you will be under oath. The inquest is held in order to determine if charges will be filed against one or both of your parents."

"Yes, Mr. Markel."

He waited, and I didn't look down. I just thought of baby blankets, of baby carriages, of soft, downy hair.

He pushed his glasses up his nose. The lenses flashed, hiding his eyes. He gave me instructions on how to speak, what to wear, how never to get angry, to stay calm no matter what. I should never look at Joe or Mom before I spoke.

"Miss Spooner — may I call you Evie? — thank you. You take mathematics in school, correct? Well, this is elementary mathematics, Evie. No additions, no subtractions. If called, you say exactly what you just said."

I nodded.

"If you are called, the state's attorney will ask if your mother was ever alone with Peter Coleridge. They will ask if your parents got along."

Yes. We'd already gone over those answers, too.

"They might ask if your mother was in love with Peter Coleridge. What will you answer, Miss Spooner?

"Miss Spooner?"

I answered the way he told me, clear and quiet.

"No," I said. I looked right at him when I said it, just the way Joe had told me to when he'd taught me how to lie. Just the way he'd looked at me when he told me he hadn't killed Peter.

I wasn't expecting the crowds. Mr. Markel had warned me but I still was surprised when I saw all the people on the stairs, waiting. I wondered what they were waiting for, and I realized it was us.

I thought there would be one reporter, but there were so many, and they asked me questions as we pushed our way up the stairs, Joe on one side of me, Mom on the other, Mr. Markel in front with Grandma Glad.

I kept my head down and my hair swung in front of my face. I thanked Mrs. Grayson for my new hairstyle.

The courtroom was the same one I'd spent the night in during the hurricane. I walked right past the bench where I'd slept. It seemed like years ago that I'd been here, scared and alone. Now the room was bright and hot, even with the fans whirring all around. I watched the blades. If I concentrated hard enough, I could lose myself in the blur.

We sat and the judge came in, stout and red-faced, with heavy black-framed glasses. Mom took my hand and held it. Hers was icy and damp, and every few moments she squeezed my fingers hard. I wished I could

228

push her hand away, but I was afraid the reporters would see me do it.

The first witness was one of the maids from Le Mirage, the young one with the nice smile. She looked apologetically at Joe and Mom as she sat down in the witness chair.

She testified that one day she'd emptied the waste-basket, and there were pieces of a pineapple vase in it.

"Something the tourists buy, you know," she said. "I felt bad, but I was glad it wasn't me who smashed it."

Joe was called next. He was nervous. What Mom called his "salesman hat" went on. He said things like "your fine state of Florida" and "this terrible tragedy" and "even in the service, you never get used to a pal dying." Which was a lie, because he told me once that the awful thing about the service was that you *did* get used to dying. *You learn it pretty quick. Never make friends with the new guy.*

He went over what happened on the boat, how they decided to go out into the ocean and how it was a dumb move, he admitted it, something that tourists do, and they were almost swamped by the waves when the engine quit.

"You said Mr. Coleridge was an experienced sailor, Mr. Spooner," the attorney said.

"He said he was."

"Were you at the helm when he attempted to fix the engine?"

"He told me to take it. He told me to keep it steady, you know. It had started to rain a bit, and we'd been out for most of the afternoon by then. The seas just kept getting higher. There was no radio. This squall came — we couldn't see more than a foot in front of us."

"Do you think your handling of the boat contributed to Mr. Coleridge's fall, Mr. Spooner?"

"Now, I've asked myself that question a thousand times, sir. I kept the boat as steady as I could. But the wind had picked up something fierce, so we were getting bounced around. When he went over, I shouted for Bev to come up with the life vests —"

"You weren't wearing them at the time?"

"Well, I was, and Bev was, but Peter said he didn't need one. We threw one overboard, right away. We thought we saw his head, we thought we could get to him. But he slipped under."

Mom bent her head.

I concentrated on the fan, whirring.

The lawyer asked in a sneery way how Joe had fixed the engine. Joe said what he did, and added that he owned appliance stores, so he was good with motors.

He wished he'd been the one to crawl down into the engine well first, he said.

"You don't know how often I wished that," he said.

You can feel a courtroom's mood if you listen hard. Rustling and coughing and murmurs and something in the air, deeper than words, that passes from person to person.

They didn't like Joe.

They didn't believe him.

There were more questions, but it was over for Joe. We heard how long he looked for Peter, how he almost capsized going back through the inlet to the lake, how he knew he'd never make it back to the dock. It was dark by then, pitch-dark, and it was just dumb luck that he got stuck in the mangroves and found a safe place to leave the boat. The voices went on and on and I was hearing them without listening. I held Mom's hand, slick with sweat.

She was next.

After that, me.

"I think I'm going to be sick," Mom whispered.

They called her name, and she walked up to the chair at the front. She looked so serious, and so pretty. She'd flattened out her curls ("No tumbling hair tomorrow," Mr. Markel had warned her yesterday) and drawn back her hair in a bun. She wore a little white hat that matched the white collar of her navy dotted-swiss dress. She crossed her legs at the ankles. Instead of sandals she wore navy pumps.

I could feel the temperature in the room change. Not how warm it was, but how people were thinking. They'd made Joe into a murderer because they wanted him to be. Now they were watching Mom. Was she his hard-boiled accomplice, was she a tramp, or was she an innocent wife chained to a jealous man? That was what they wanted her to tell them.

I wanted to know the answers, too. But not here. Not like this.

Mom answered the questions so quietly that the judge had to ask her to speak up three times. I don't know where she had put her pizzazz. Maybe she had squashed it in that little lace-trimmed pocket of her dress.

She told the same story Joe had. Except she added some other feelings. She said she hadn't wanted to go, but she wanted to be a "good sport."

"Did your husband and Peter Coleridge get along?"

"Oh, yes. They were chums. You know, there aren't many tourists here this time of year, so you get to know the people at the hotel."

"Did you have romantic feelings for Mr. Coleridge?"

"I have romantic feelings for my husband," Mom said firmly, and you could tell the courtroom liked that.

"A witness has testified that he saw you leaving in Mr. Coleridge's car every day."

"With my daughter," Mom corrected with such gentleness that I could feel the spectators move slightly to her side. "He took us for drives sometimes."

I sneaked a look around. Everybody's eyes were on her. Nobody was whispering or scratching or blowing their nose.

She told the courtroom about the pineapple vase. Yes, she'd been to the store with Peter. She'd been walking to town and he gave her a lift. It was the nice thing to do, he was that sort of person.

And how did the vase get smashed?

I felt myself almost falling, I was so afraid. Mom tilted her head and gave the tiniest shrug.

"My husband and I were dancing to the radio, and we bumped into it," she said. She looked over at Joe and smiled just a little bit. "He's not a very good dancer."

A woman in back of me laughed a little, and the judge banged his gavel.

When did my mother get to be such a cool liar? When did she learn to use her face to look so innocent?

Maybe when she fell in love with Peter. She had so many lies to tell.

The attorney in the gray suit started pounding her with questions now. He didn't like the way the tide was turning. What time did they get the boat, whose idea was it to leave the lake and go out into the ocean, did the two men argue?

"The wind picked up. There were these gusts . . . they frightened me. Peter said if he couldn't fix it, we could be in trouble. The boat went up like this —" Mom held her hand out and tilted it. "I was terrified. So I went downstairs."

Everyone in the courtroom busted out laughing.

"You went below," the attorney said in a scolding way, like she hadn't done her nautical homework and he'd caught her out.

"Below." Mom nodded like an eager student. I think if she'd smiled, if she'd laughed along with everyone, that would have ruined it. They wouldn't have liked it if she was in on the joke.

He kept asking questions, but Mom had won. They liked her now. She was from New York but she didn't know what they knew. She had turned herself from a femme fatale into a dumb blonde. They knew she couldn't kill anyone. She was too pretty. She was too dim.

Chapter 31

"You both did well," Mr. Markel said. We'd left the courtroom straight through the judge's chambers to avoid all the cameras. Now we sat in a small office Mr. Markel had borrowed. Miss Geiger had left us lunch. Sandwiches had been unwrapped and a thermos of coffee sat steaming, its lid forgotten. The only one who ate and drank was Grandma Glad.

"Evie's next up, right?" Joe asked, leaning forward, his hands clasped. "And she's the last witness. It could all be over today, right?"

"There's another witness," Mr. Markel said. "Just came forward. Walter Forrest."

"Who?" Joe asked.

Mr. Markel looked down at his file. "He worked at Le Mirage. As a bellhop and valet."

"Wally?" I asked.

"What the devil does Wally know about anything?" Joe asked.

Mr. Markel looked over his glasses at Joe. "That, indeed, is the question."

Mom pushed her chair back and went to the window. She hugged herself as she looked down at the street.

"Is there anything you can think of that Mr. Forrest might have to say?" Mr. Markel asked.

"Nothing," Joe said. "Bev?"

"Nothing," she said. She didn't turn around.

Wally was wearing a white shirt tight at the neck and a bow tie. His pants were hitched up too high. When he sat down I could see his brown socks end and his calf begin. He didn't look at me or Joe or Mom.

I recognized his father in the courtroom. He kept his hands on his knees and his eyes on his boy.

Wally stated his name and where he worked. He said he was acquainted with the Spooners and with Mr. Coleridge, that he parked cars for the hotel and carried suitcases and ran errands. "Short staff, they didn't usually open in September, see," he said. "They don't get so many guests. So sure, you get to know 'em."

And why did Walter come forward and talk to the police, Mr. Toomer wanted to know, asking the question in a smug way that let you know he was delighted he knew the answer before everyone else.

"I walk home on the lake trail," Wally said. "Every night, the same way. It's real quiet now because it's off-season. Mr. Wentworth's place — he lives down the block from the hotel — it backs up on the lake there, and I cut through it to get to the trail. It's a shortcut. He gave me permission, since he eats at the hotel most every night during the season."

"Mr. Allen Wentworth," the attorney said, and I could tell everyone knew who he was, some Palm Beach swell.

"Anyway," Wally said, swallowing so hard I could see it from the third row, "one night, it was a Friday, because I get off later on Fridays, I was walking through the grass, and I hear something, I don't know what, so I stop. And I walk over a little bit . . ." Wally began to squirm in his chair and stuck a finger in his collar. "Ah, and I see a couple leaning against a tree."

"What was the couple doing?"

"They were, ah, necking, sir."

"Could you identify the people you saw, Walter?"

"Well, I recognized Mrs. Spooner right off, because of that blue gown she's got. And she must have heard me, because she twisted around, but she didn't see me. She ducked her face kind of, and the guy looked over her shoulder, and I saw it was Mr. Coleridge."

"You're certain?"

"Yessir, I saw them plain as day."

The judge knocked the gavel for silence.

I knew exactly which night it was. Mom had gone upstairs with a headache. I'd sat in the lobby for a while and then gone outside, and Peter had been walking to his car. We'd gone to the beach.

He kissed me that night.

But first, he'd kissed Mom. I remembered seeing Wally in the lobby, just getting off his shift. I'd killed at least ten minutes after that, walking around the hotel. All that time, Mom and Peter were together.

She didn't go upstairs that night. She didn't have a headache. She'd run out the side door, the same door I'd used so no one would see me. She'd met him under the trees. They'd arranged it beforehand. And Wally had caught them.

"What did you do next?"

"I walked away. Real quiet. I didn't want to get in any trouble. The thing is, about hotels, my old boss, Mr. Forney, told me, whatever happens in a hotel you keep your mouth shut. Whatever you see, you keep your mouth shut. That's the way you keep your job, he said. So I didn't say anything."

"Why did you come forward, Walter?"

"When I read the news, I told my dad what I saw. It

was him who told me to come forward. It's the right thing to do, he said."

"Indeed," the state's attorney said in a flowery way, as if he was reciting the Gettysburg Address. "Indeed."

He let the silence hang while he pretended to look down at his notes. We kept our eyes straight forward, because everyone in the courtroom was trying to get a good look at us.

"Now, let's go to the early morning of September seventeenth. You were working at the hotel that night."

Wally nodded eagerly, a question he could answer without getting anybody in trouble. "I was on bellhop and valet duty. Nobody was up yet, just a couple guests. Mr. Spooner came down and asked for his car, so I brought it around. Usually he'd just take off, but that morning he shot the breeze a little. We were all talking about the storm by then. Wondering where it would hit. And he asked about hurricane preparations for the hotel, what we did to prepare and whatnot. And then he asks about the boats, what happens to the boats."

The courtroom was completely silent. The judge didn't have to bang his gavel.

"Said he heard something about hurricane holes. So I tell him, sure, there are places to tie a boat, hope nothing bad happens, a kind of shelter. Bunch of them down by Lake Worth, some a little bit north. I told him about snook fishing around Munyon Island, that my dad has a boat. He's interested in that, asks if my dad rents his boat, and I say sure, that's what he does for a living. So he says that maybe he'd want to take it out that morning, and he'd make it worth my dad's while. I don't think anything about it until I hear that he found a hurricane hole for the boat. That's all." Wally looked at the attorney in a pleading way, waiting to be released.

I could feel it on the back of my neck. I knew the whispers would travel from those in the courtroom to those out in the hall, and then to those down the courthouse steps, and through the streets of downtown. I could feel it in the eagerness of the reporters as they jostled to get pictures of Mom.

Joe had planned it, they thought now. The whole thing. He'd planned the murder for right before the storm. He'd planned to stay out with the boat, he'd planned to hide it. Maybe he'd even done something to the engine, somehow. Whatever had happened, every single person in the courtroom now knew that Joe was a murderer, and Mom was a tramp.

They were guilty now.

*　　*　　*

We had already learned how to walk past photographers, head turned in, keep walking no matter what, don't stop for anything, keep going toward Mr. Markel's open car door, slip inside. Mom first, then Joe. We'd sent Grandma Glad out the back door with Miss Geiger. I was last in the car and I tripped and fell halfway inside. Joe picked me up by the wrist and hauled me in and I lay sprawled over their ankles while he slammed the door shut and Mr. Markel took off.

Joe leaned over and helped me up, and I slid between them. We didn't talk.

I couldn't look at my mother. I couldn't stand the smell of her perfume. I kept myself very still so that I wouldn't brush against her. I couldn't bear the picture in my head of her pressed against Peter.

After Wally's testimony, I'd felt how the mood had changed in the courtroom. Now everyone wanted to punish her. Because she was beautiful, because she was careless, because she was bad. I wanted to punish her, too.

After a minute, Joe placed his hand over mine, so gently. His hand needed my hand. I could feel it in his fingers, his worried fingers. I slipped my hand away.

Chapter 32

"I had a headache, I went out for some air, and he was there," Mom said. "He said, come look at this palace across the street, you can't believe it. Then he made a pass. I pushed him away, I didn't want to be rude. I said, 'Down, boy' or some such. That Wally kid got it all wrong. That's all."

We sat together, Mom and me on the couch, Joe in the armchair. Grandma Glad sat on the edge of the bed, her arms folded.

"They're going to hang me for it," Joe said. He didn't look at Mom. "That was all they needed."

"She's the one who should hang," Grandma Glad said.

"That's enough!" Mom's voice rose on the *enough*. She sprang up, her fists clenched at her sides. "I've had it, old lady. This is my husband, not yours. I don't need you sticking your nose in our business."

"You need me in your business!" Grandma Glad

snapped. "You see what happens when I'm not around? You see what you do to him? You can twist him around your pinky finger in your fancy nail polish, Miss High and Mighty, but I know the truth. You can put sawdust on the floor, but a fish store still stinks like fish!"

Mom looked like she wanted to leap over the coffee table and wrap her hands around Grandma Glad's throat. "You wouldn't know the truth if you tripped and landed in it nose first, Gladys. I love Joe and I'm not going anywhere. Unless he sends me away." She looked Joe full in the face, and for the first time since we left the courthouse, he met her eyes.

"Unless you send me away," she said to him. Her voice broke.

Joe stood. "Ma, could you leave us alone for a few minutes? Go on down to the lobby, order yourself some coffee."

Grandma Glad blinked. "What?"

"They have some nice pastries down there. Have a little rest."

"You're kicking me out?"

Joe stood his ground. "I need to talk to my family."

"*I'm* your family!"

Joe walked to the door and opened it. "Just a half hour."

Grandma Glad couldn't refuse. She picked up her big purse. She walked out, furious. Her face was dark red. After all these years complaining about her blood pressure, she finally had a problem.

Joe closed the door after her. He and Mom just looked at each other for the longest moment.

"This is how it's going to be from now on," Joe said in a dead voice. "After this is over, when we get home, we never say his name again."

Mom nodded. "Yes, Joe."

"The only way I can do this is if it's like the war. I come home and I forget it."

"Yes."

He crossed over and put his hands on her shoulders and shook her. "You get it?" he said through his teeth.

Mom's careful French twist came down from its pins. "Yes, Joe."

With every exclamation, he shook her again. "And I'm going to buy us a *house*, and we're going to *live* and be *happy*. That's what's going to happen!"

He dropped Mom's shoulders and she fell back on the couch. I was pressed against the corner.

Joe shook his head, his eyes closed. Then he turned and walked out. The door slammed behind him.

Mom's face was tight and scared. Her hair was half pinned up, half falling down. "Accessory to murder," she said. "That's what they'll charge me with. That's the least it will be."

She held her head in her hands and rocked. "Do you know what this means? A trial. Disgrace and ruin and prison. And worse for Joe. They'll hang him. What did I do?" She started to cry in jerks, her breath coming sharp and painful. "What did I do?"

I didn't move. I sat and waited until she was almost quiet.

She crawled over to me on the couch. She put her hands on my cheeks.

"You and me," she whispered.

I couldn't answer her.

"Stick like glue. Stick like glue, Evie!"

I couldn't finish it. I couldn't give her that. I couldn't go back to the place where we'd been.

It rained that night, all night, a soft pattering rain. There was no wind, so we kept the windows open. It must have cleared after midnight because a breeze came through, bringing the smell of the ocean, strong and tangy. I had the bed to myself. Grandma Glad had made a big show of getting her own room, to make a point that nobody cared about. So the three of us slept in the same room, or didn't sleep, our breaths mixing all together, in and out.

It was that night.

The match snapped, then sizzled, and I woke up fast. I heard my mother inhale as she took a long pull on a cigarette. Her lips stuck on the filter, so I knew she was still wearing lipstick. She'd been up all night.

She lay on the bed next to me. I felt her fingers on my hair and I kept sleep-breathing. I risked a look under my eyelashes.

She was in her pink nightgown, ankles crossed, head flung back against the pillows. Arm in the air, elbow bent, cigarette glowing in her fingers. Tanned legs glistening in the darkness. Blond hair tumbling past her shoulders.

I breathed in smoke and My Sin perfume. It was her smell. It filled the air.

I didn't move, but I could tell she knew I was awake. I kept on pretending to be asleep. She pretended not to know.

I breathed in and out, perfume and smoke, perfume and smoke, and we lay like that for a long time, until I heard the seagulls crying, sadder than a funeral, and I knew it was almost morning.

I tipped over the empty bottle of soda and anchored it in the sand.

I'd gone over it all in my head, and I still didn't know.

I remembered all the things I'd seen. It was all there in my head, the things that happened, the things we said.

I should stay away from you, pussycat.

Me? I'm just a softy.

I wish a lot of things, and one of them is, I wish you were back in that house, with your battle-axe Grandma Glad.

The rest of us, we have to figure out how to break the rules.

Where does she go, Evie?

I like to blow horns. Nice and loud, so everyone can hear.

Let me put it this way: I think he'd be a hell of a lot happier if I disappeared.

Tom told me I should look them up in New York. Now that I've got old times to talk about with them.

You're not the type of guy to hold a grudge, are you?

What did I do?

If I could add up the clues, would I know the truth? Would I know if Joe had planned to kill Peter? Did everything that added up for Joe — jealousy and fear and spite — make him think, yeah, this was his only answer? Or maybe he hadn't planned it. Maybe out on that pounding ocean he found his answer. Maybe Mom was "downstairs" and didn't see it. Maybe she did. Maybe she was so mad at Peter for double-timing her with me that she helped.

No. If I knew one thing, I knew that Mom didn't do it. She put her hands over her ears during thunderstorms.

The ashtray had flown through the air and shattered. Her face had been so blank.

How could I know what she was capable of? I'd seen what regular ordinary men could do. I'd seen newsreels of what they found after the war.

But I'd never thought about it before. The magazines and movies told me different, that the war was over and we were all okey-dokey, drinking Cokes and smoking Camels and saving up for the new Chevrolet.

Joe was part of that. He came back from the war and hit the ground running. I'd admired that, how the very next day he started making calls. I didn't know then what he was doing, how late at night he'd talk to Gladys, both of them with glasses of whiskey, talking low. And we were all so full of happiness because he was home that nobody thought twice.

"Let them have their time," Mom had said. "There's plenty of Joe to go around now."

He'd wanted success so badly that he'd stolen and he'd lied. How bad did he want to keep it?

If I lined up the reasons for Joe to be guilty, I could see them clear as morning. But if he was telling the truth, it just meant he looked guilty, not that he was. Sure, he'd asked Wally about the hurricane hole. But Joe was the type of guy who was interested in whatever he didn't know. He was always asking the mailman about what were the most comfortable shoes, or the milkman about how he got up so early.

Would Mom stay with him if she knew he was a murderer? She didn't seem scared of him. She seemed scared of him going away.

Could it really happen like this? That a girl like you can make me feel . . .

Make you feel what?

Make me feel.

What did I owe you, Peter?

Truth and justice? If judges would judge, if lawyers wouldn't trick, if reporters would tell what really happened instead of what sold papers.

Fat chance.

Truth, justice . . . I always thought they were absolutes, like God. And Mom. And apple pie.

But you could make apple pie from Ritz crackers. You could make cakes without sugar. We learned how to fake things, during the war.

What did loyalty mean? Loyalty to the family, to the church, to the neighborhood, to the Brooklyn Dodgers. Why did loyalty stop there? Why didn't it keep on going? It didn't seem to take a spin around the whole world, that was for sure.

I wished I could get one clean breath from this humid air. I wanted the snap of autumn, blue sky clear and deep, the familiar cracks of the sidewalks, my feet jumping so surely over them, never missing. I wanted to go home so badly.

I touched the place on my temple that her lips always found, ever since I was a baby. Did everything funnel down to that one delicate place, the place where love was?

Chapter 33

Mom had bought four new dresses, all of them dark colors. I picked out a navy dress she hadn't worn yet, with a narrow belt and a little matching jacket. I took out white and navy high-heeled spectator pumps from a brand-new box. I slipped them on. They hurt.

I brushed my hair with hard strokes and drew it back off my forehead. I twisted it and put in the pins like an expert. I rolled up the tube of Fatal Apple lipstick and painted my mouth.

I looked like a doll, a dish. The image in the mirror — it wasn't me.

If I had the clothes and the walk, I could make up a whole new person. I wasn't who I used to be, anyway. A different me would do the thing I had to do today. The dish would do it.

"Evie?" Mom was awake now, groping for her first

cigarette. She got a good look at me, and she sat straight up. "What are you doing?"

Her panicked voice woke up Joe.

I looked at them, in separate beds, the sheets tangled and twisting onto the floor. I saw a purplish bruise on Mom's arm, right where Joe had grabbed her.

Wobbling a little bit in the too-tight shoes, I walked out.

I couldn't explain, you see. I couldn't tell her that I understood just a little better what Peter was talking about when he talked about war. I found out that what you think is necessary, what you have to do — well, all of a sudden, that can cover plenty of new ground.

It's just a matter of what you're willing to do.

Noise and heat slamming against my ears. Camera shutters clicking. People yelling. Sun hitting my eyes, glinting off metal like shards of glass flying.

They thought Joe was guilty now, so the sidewalk in front of the courthouse was filled. So were the stairs and the hallways. Reporters and photographers lunged forward, flashbulbs popping like gunshots.

The instructions were clear. The three of us were to link arms and walk up the stairs to the courtroom.

"Don't stop, whatever you do," Mr. Markel had ordered

us in the car. "Don't stop to look at anyone — just keep walking."

We all looked at his narrow back in his brown suit as he used his shoulders and his walk to clear the way. Our pipsqueak attorney had turned into a pretty decent linebacker.

We didn't look at each other. I had showed up at the last minute with Mr. Markel, and there was no time to talk to Mom and Joe. Their fear was in the car with us. I wouldn't meet Mom's scared eyes.

We walked hard and fast, our sides pressed together. My navy straw hat was pulled over my eyes, shadowing my face.

Didja do it, Joe?

Did she help you do it?

Didja love him, Bev?

Repent, sinners! There is one almighty judge and his name is Jesus!

They called us Joe and Bev and Evelyn. The photographers said, *Evelyn, turn this way* and *Aw, come on, Bev, give us a look over here.* Like we were pals.

Not even my teachers called me Evelyn. I would give them Evelyn. Someone with cool hands and a confident walk.

I tried to make the noise into one blur of sound. I thought about the Third Avenue El. We hardly ever took it because Mom was afraid of it. She didn't like subways either — she closed her eyes almost the whole time. After all, her parents had died in a train crash. It was me who had to watch out for the stops.

I always wanted to take the El. The train raced above the avenue, and you could see right into apartment windows, especially if it was getting dark and lights were on. Just a quick look, like a snapshot someone snatches away from your hand. A man in his undershirt eating at a table. A woman putting on her hat. Someone sleeping in a chair. Down below you, noise had a shadow. Under the tracks there was the roar of the train, and then the echo of the roar, and then the bounce of it against the buildings. But you were in the middle of it, way above. You weren't part of the city; you were cutting right through the heart of it.

We turned into the courtroom.

It was so humid inside that the windows had steamed over. People stood in back and down the side aisles. They all craned their necks as we walked toward our seats. We sat in the first row, right in back of the counsel table. Mr. Markel left us there and nodded at the other attorney. He opened his briefcase.

I had called him from the phone in the lobby that morning. He'd met me at his office. Early, before Miss Geiger came to work. I'd told him what I was going to say and he didn't interrupt, just took notes on a yellow pad. When I'd finished, he'd closed it and looked up.

"Are you sure?"

I'd nodded.

"Do you have a handkerchief with you?" he'd asked. "Use it."

I felt their eyes on my back as the judge came in. Their curiosity was like a wild, living thing in the room. I had to keep wiping my hands on my skirt because I wanted to be Evelyn with cool hands, not Evie with her stomach in knots and sweat snaking from her armpits. I was concentrating so hard on being cool that I missed them calling my name. Joe had to nudge me.

I stood up so quickly that my purse fell on the floor and I tripped on it. Bad start.

I walked my new walk, the one I had because of the tight high heels, my hips swaying. *Chin up!* I heard Mrs. Grayson say in my head.

I looked up at the judge, then back down in my lap. I needed that judge on my side. I needed to keep my hands and my stomach calm. I needed not to be sick. I needed not to faint. I had to do this today, because if I had to come back tomorrow, I couldn't do it. I couldn't be Evelyn for one more day.

I put my hand on the Bible.

I swear it on a stack of Bibles. We said it back home

when we told the truth, no fudging. Because if you swore on a Bible and you lie, you'd go to straight to hell on the downtown express.

Mr. Markel rose. He told me in a warm tone I'd never heard from him before not to be nervous. I nodded nervously.

"Just tell the truth," he said. "Let's start the night of September fifth. What happened that evening?"

"We were all having dinner in the restaurant at the hotel."

"You're sure it was that evening?"

"Yes, it was a Friday night. We'd been to the movies that day."

"Who was there that evening, Miss Spooner?"

"My father and mother, and the Graysons, and Peter — Mr. Coleridge. After dinner was over, the ladies decided they'd go upstairs to their rooms, and the gentlemen would go to the lobby for coffee. Peter leaned over and asked me if I'd go for a walk, and I said yes." I hesitated. "But I didn't tell my parents."

"Why is that, Miss Spooner?"

It was hard for me to avoid looking at Joe and Mom at that moment. But I remembered Mr. Markel's instructions. I wasn't going to slip.

"Because I knew they'd say no. They thought Peter was too old for me."

"Was it the first time you'd met Mr. Coleridge without your parents' consent?"

"No." I whispered the word, and the judge made me say it again.

"You were, in fact, carrying on a secret romance with the deceased?"

"Yes, sir. It started when Peter drove me and my mother places. If we were alone for a minute or two, he would ask me to meet him later. If I was able to, I did."

The crowd was completely silent now. They hung on every word.

"Did your mother have any knowledge of this?"

"No, sir."

"Did you ever go to the house he had used?"

"Yes. I didn't know he'd broken in."

"What did you do on the night in question?"

"First I went upstairs. I could hear my mother getting ready for bed. While she was in the bathroom, I went to her closet and took out one of her dresses. The blue one, because that was the prettiest."

A flashbulb popped, and the judge ordered the photographer out of the courtroom.

"I wanted to look older. So I met him in my mother's dress, and we walked for a bit, and then we stopped under this tree, and we kissed. He thought he heard someone coming, and he pressed my head against his shirt. A minute later he saw someone go by. He didn't know it was Wally, but he promised me that whoever it was hadn't seen my face."

"Do you think he was telling the truth?"

"Oh, yes. Because I heard the footsteps, too. And we were hidden by the tree, so the person couldn't have seen us until he was pretty close."

"What happened next?"

"We waited just a little bit, and then he walked me back to the road. I sneaked back into the hotel. My mother was sleeping by then, so I put the dress back in her closet."

"Did the dress fit you?"

"Yes, perfectly. My mother and I are the same size."

"Were you in love with Mr. Coleridge, Miss Spooner?"

I ducked my head. "Yes, sir, I was."

At least I got to tell one solid truth today.

"Did you have any knowledge at any time that Mr. Coleridge might have a romance with your mother?"

"Oh, no. I knew he didn't. She spent time with both of us. It was a good . . . cover, Peter said. No one would suspect the two of us if my mother was along."

"Was Peter Coleridge in love with you, Miss Spooner?"

"Yes. He was. He told me so."

Mom slowly slid off her chair.

The photographers who were hiding their cameras rushed forward. The judge banged his gavel, but no one listened. I stood up.

"Give her some air!" I heard Joe shout.

People rushed forward, but Joe waved them back. The judge banged his gavel again. Someone called for water. It had turned into a circus in a tent, all color and heat and movement. And smell. I felt like I could smell everyone in the room, the ladies with the half-moons of perspiration under the arms of their rayon dresses, the men with their handkerchiefs already wet from mopping their foreheads, their hats tilted back.

Through all the commotion, I noticed a man sitting on the aisle near the back. I noticed him by his stillness. He was the only one not whispering or craning his neck to see Mom. A man dressed in a plain dark suit, a white shirt buttoned tightly at his neck, and no tie. He would have been handsome if it weren't for the deep lines in his face, his thinning iron-gray hair. I thought I was used to people staring at me, but this gaze felt deeper than the others.

"I call for a recess, your honor," Mr. Markel said.

The judge sighed. He leaned over and said to me, "Would you like a recess, miss?"

"No, I'd like to go on," I said.

"Then please sit down, Miss Spooner."

I turned again to Mr. Markel, in a hurry to get this over with. I could still feel the gray-haired man's gaze.

Mom pushed away the glass of water one of the court officers kept trying to get her to drink. She pressed her handkerchief against her forehead. She looked so pale, so small.

I broke Mr. Markel's rule and looked straight into her eyes. She shook her head, just a little bit, tears pooling in her eyes. I didn't know what the head shake meant. *You don't have to lie, Evie?*

But I did, and she knew it, so maybe she was shaking her head at the whole awful stink of it.

Not too much longer, Mom.

"Did your parents ever find out about your romance with Peter Coleridge?" Mr. Markel asked.

"I told them this morning," I said.

"They were surprised?"

"They were shocked. I wish I'd told them before."

"Now we come to the second part of your testimony," Mr. Markel said. "I know you come forward reluctantly on this issue, Miss Spooner, and I know this might be hard for you. Can you tell us about the events of September seventeenth?"

"Well, my parents and Peter had planned to hire a

boat that day. Then we found out that a storm was coming, and they talked about whether to go."

"There were small craft warnings."

"Peter said he could handle the boat, if they still wanted to go."

The man with the thin gray hair and the thick hands was still staring at me.

Stop looking at me like that, stop it.

"So they went out on Mr. Forrest's boat, and I was waiting for them at the hotel. Wally — Walter — was getting off his shift."

"That's Walter Forrest, the former bellhop at the Le Mirage Hotel?"

"Yes. I was nervous and upset — the weather was getting worse, and I was worried about my parents and Peter. I knew Wally from the hotel, and he seemed like a swell boy. He reassured me, saying the weather wasn't too bad yet. Then he said maybe we should walk to the beach and look at the waves. We walked along the beach for a while, and then ... he suggested that we sit up near the dunes."

"Was anyone else on the beach at that time?"

"No, it was beginning to get quite windy."

"What happened then?"

I hesitated.

"Miss Spooner," Mr. Markel said in a gentle voice, "please go on."

"Well, Wally kissed me. And I guess he lost his head. He pushed me down on the sand. He . . . pulled up my skirt. I tried to get him off me —"

Just the fans whirring now. That was the only noise. It was like a roar in my ears. I had to speak through the noise. I saw a woman in the third row, her round blue eyes trained on my face. I saw sympathy there, and surprise, and . . . greed.

"I'm sure he didn't mean to frighten me —"

Suddenly Mr. Forrest rose from a middle row. I hadn't seen him. His big sunburned face was red. "Liar! You led him on! You're a whore like your mother!"

The word *whore* was like a bomb thrown into the courtroom. A couple of women shrieked, and Joe half-rose, as if he'd deck Captain Sandy, and the judge called, "Get that man out of my courtroom!"

Whore. How strange it felt, to have that word thrown at my head.

I had to concentrate on the roar of the train in my head, of the shadow that noise could cast.

The silent man on the aisle, watching me. Never taking his eyes off me.

I leaned over and buried my face in my handkerchief. I wasn't crying. Tears were so far away from me now, it was like they were in another country. I just kept my head there, until the gavel stopped banging and the room went quiet, and I knew that Mr. Forrest had been escorted from the courtroom.

"Miss Spooner?" The judge spoke in a nicer voice than I'd heard before. "Can you continue?"

Slowly, I raised my head. The women had stopped fanning themselves. The reporters were furiously scribbling in their notebooks and looking at me at the same time.

Everything happens underneath the same moon. Things you never thought you'd see. Or do.

I was sorry about Wally. But I had to do it. I had to tell them what happened so that they wouldn't believe him over me. But I couldn't let it stay like that.

"I'm responsible for what happened," I said. "I went with Wally to the beach alone. And when he suggested we find a place in the dunes, I went with him. And when he kissed me, at first I was so surprised that I didn't say no. I guess he thought . . . well, I guess he thought I was fast. I don't blame him for that."

"What happened after the . . . incident?" Mr. Markel asked.

"He walked me back to the hotel. My skirt was torn. I was upset. And the hotel manager, Mr. Forney, he saw us. He was outside. He called to Wally, and later on Mr. Forney told me that he fired Wally because of what happened. It's not like I think Wally would hold a grudge against my family or anything. . . ." I looked down at my twisted handkerchief. "I mean, I hope he doesn't blame me for his getting fired. He saw someone with Peter that night, and I guess he thought it was my mother. It's not like he was making anything up. He just got confused because of the blue dress, maybe."

It was almost over. I looked out at the woman in the third row. She was nodding just a little bit as she listened.

The state's attorney was looking down at his notes. His bald spot was shiny with sweat. It was his turn now.

I answered every question, and he couldn't rattle me. He tried to do his job, but I knew by his eyes that he believed me, too. After ten minutes he gave up, and I was dismissed.

When I walked down the aisle to leave, I had to pass the man. I looked right into his face. His eyes were light green. I could see how handsome he'd been once. He had the hands of a fisherman, thick and useful-looking.

He had a way of looking at you, like he could get the full measure of you in one long glance. Peter must have inherited that. Now I faltered as his father took me in, and I felt afraid. I wanted to say something, but what?

I'm sorry.

I loved your son.

I wanted justice for him, too.

I'd answered every question, I'd thrown mud at a good boy's reputation, I'd lied, I'd been called a whore. But it was that one man's wave of contempt that finally made the tears come.

Chapter 34

**VERDICT IN COLERIDGE CASE IS
ACCIDENTAL DEATH BY DROWNING**
Joseph and Beverly Spooner Exonerated

———

Lack of Evidence for Trial, Rules Judge Friend

We were packed and on the road by noon.

It was a long way home, and a long way to go without talking. Grandma Glad and I shared the backseat, keeping a careful distance, even when we slept. She sat with her feet planted on either side of her brown valise, and she never moved or complained, even when the sweat dripped off her nose onto her bust. She wouldn't talk to Mom, and Mom wouldn't talk to her, and I didn't know if Joe and Mom were talking to each other.

The miles ticked off under the car wheels. The weather got cooler, and we had to dig for sweaters. We never looked at each other. We looked at Georgia and South Carolina, North Carolina, and Virginia. Maryland. Delaware. New Jersey.

When nobody looked at you, it made it so easy to feel like you'd disappeared.

All the way on the drive, I just wanted to get home, but when we got there on Saturday morning, there was something that made me and Mom both stop in the driveway and look up at the house, hesitate about going in. I'd been thinking of my room, and my bed, and the white bedspread, and my own pillow. I hadn't been thinking that I was going back to Grandma Glad's house, a place that had never really been mine.

Mom and I looked at each other, really looked at each other, for the first time since Florida. Then she gave a little tilt to her head and shrugged. She picked up her suitcase and walked up the path. I remembered the night in the car when she'd tilted the rearview mirror and put her lipstick on. How she made herself do it.

Being an adult — was this it? Doing the thing you most in your life didn't want to do, and doing it with a shrug?

I picked up my suitcase and followed her. Grandma Glad was already on the porch, her hand tightly gripping her valise. Joe slipped the key into the lock. We stepped into the dark hall. Every house has a smell, but you can't smell it if it's your own home. I could smell Grandma Glad's house.

Grandma Glad went up the stairs and I followed her. She turned into her room and I stopped, waiting. I peeked through the door. She stood, looking around for a minute, then opened the closet door and put the valise on the top shelf, grunting while she did it. As she closed the closet I scooted down to my room next door.

I hadn't even finished unpacking when Margie arrived. Thanks, no doubt, to Mrs. Clancy's gossip know-how. I knew as soon as she saw our car that she'd pick up the phone.

I could see in a moment what Margie wanted, how greedily she greeted me, how her eyes swept over my hair and my figure.

"Tell me everything," she said dramatically. "It was in the paper here, you know. My mother said it was an ordeal for your stepfather. An ordeal, she said. But then you said it was you all along who loved him. An older man!"

I felt my lips close. There weren't any words I wanted to use to talk to Margie.

She had been my best friend for six years. There were all of the secrets we'd whispered, sweaters we'd borrowed, homework we'd done together at her kitchen table. I'd been practically adopted by her mother, brought into family dinners and stickball games, hoeing their Victory Garden, washing their big old '39 Ford with Margie on sunny Saturday afternoons.

I didn't want to be her friend anymore.

She settled herself on my bed and smoothed out her skirt. "You can tell me," she said. She lifted her face to me, all expectation. She would have the gossip before anyone.

It would certainly increase my standing in the cafeteria. I would no longer hover there with my tray, looking for an empty seat. Girls would slide over to make room for me. For us. Margie would be by my side, the interpreter of what had happened to me. I could see her mouth moving, I could see it all, my story served up on a tray with the grilled cheese.

Now I have a story, Peter.

"I don't want to talk about it," I said.

"But —"

"I have to unpack." I said the words so curtly that she reared back, her cheeks red.

"Well, honestly! You don't have to be so rude!"

I reached over and took a blue skirt out of the suitcase. I smoothed it and put it on the hanger carefully. By the time I hung it up, Margie had gone.

Chapter 35

On Sunday morning, I saw Ruthie Kalman come out of the drugstore as I was heading to the subway. She speeded up when she saw me. I almost had to run to catch up.

"Ruthie!" My breath came out in a cloud of steam. It was cooler today, a fall day as crisp as an apple.

She turned slightly and said hello while she kept walking.

I matched my steps to hers.

"Ruthie. Please stop walking."

I knew she didn't want to, but she did.

"How are you, Evie?" she asked in a flat voice.

"Terrible. How are you?"

I saw a smile tug at the corners of her mouth.

"I can hear you in chorus," I said. "You have a nice voice."

"Yeah? You do, too."

"Maybe one day we could go to the record store together. Do you like Sinatra?"

"He's okay. I don't get all swoony about him, like some girls."

"Well. I'm not the swoony type. Maybe you could tell me who you like. And we could listen to some songs."

"Maybe."

"Good."

Ruthie's gaze moved to the bag in my hand. "Are you running away?"

"No," I said. "Not today."

I knew how hotels worked now. I knew it would be okay to walk into the lobby, go to the front desk, and give a name. A telephone would be lifted, a name would be said into the phone, and the clerk would say, "Go right up." Or not.

Still I hesitated on Forty-eighth Street. Right now Mom would be making lunch. Joe would be home. Grandma Glad would still be at Mass. Joe told her last night that he'd be looking for a house for us, and she'd be staying behind. She wasn't talking to anyone at the moment. Maybe the phone would be ringing, neighbors calling up now that we were home. Everyone knowing what happened but not asking about it, wanting to be the first to hear the real story.

When the doorman started looking at me funny, I pushed open the door to the Metropole. The lobby was busy, people checking in, people checking out. Newspaper stand, bellhops pushing carts, elevators dinging. People dressed up and ready for a Sunday in New York. Other people pushing through the doors and going into the swanky-looking restaurant.

So this was what a real hotel was like.

A bellhop offered to take my bag but I shook my head. I went to the front desk and waited while the desk clerk gave a couple directions to Toffenetti's. Then he turned to me.

"Mrs. Grayson, please," I said.

"Is she expecting you?"

"No. But she knows me. Could you tell her that Evie Spooner is here to see her?"

He picked up the house phone and dialed. I waited, trying not to squirm.

"No answer," he said after a minute.

"Can I wait?" I couldn't have come this far without seeing her.

He looked at me and I saw him soften. "I know where she is. Eddie will take you up to the roof."

"The roof?"

He smiled. "The roof. Take the elevator bank to your right."

It was yes-miss and watch-your-step and thank-you-miss and going-up-miss all the way through the lobby and onto the elevator.

"The roof, please," I said.

The elevator man looked over to the desk, and the clerk gave a quick nod.

"Right away, miss." The doors swished closed. I felt the pull in my stomach as it rose. My hands were damp inside my gloves.

"Here you are, miss. Go to your right, and take the third door on your left."

I stepped out. The carpet here was thin and brown, not like the green one I'd sunk into in the lobby. I walked past the doors. One of them said TAILOR and I surprised a maid coming out, still tying on her apron.

She smiled at me. "Looking for Mrs. Grayson?"

At my nod, she led me a little way down the hall and opened the door marked ROOF.

"Go right on up."

I found narrow concrete stairs and an iron railing painted dull red. I pushed at the door and stepped onto the tar surface of the roof.

The first thing I saw was the sign, twenty feet high, maybe thirty, and with lightbulbs all screwed in. HOTEL

METROPOLE. Behind it, skyscrapers bristled, and I could make out the green rectangle of Central Park.

Mrs. Grayson sat on a camp stool a few feet away, painting at an easel. Her dark hair was in a ponytail, and she wore a smock over a turtleneck sweater and slim trousers. Flat shoes were on her feet. I picked my way past the air vents toward her. When she saw me, she opened her mouth in a comical O of surprise. She laughed as she stood up. I could see how happy she was to see me, and my nervousness lifted a little bit.

"Evie! What a lovely surprise. Come look at this mess I'm doing."

I stepped over to look at her canvas. She was painting the view, tall buildings and the park, all in thick black lines and blue shadows going every which way. Tiny squares of gold marched up and down in vertical rows.

She was right, it looked like a mess.

"I like it," I said.

"You sweet liar. It's not good, but I keep trying."

"That's what you did in Florida — you painted. When you'd go off by yourself."

"Sketching, actually. Do you want to go down to the apartment and get some tea, or stay up here?"

I was dying to see the Graysons' apartment, but I felt better up here in the cold fresh air.

"Up here, please."

"Oh, good. I was hoping you'd say that." She tossed her smock on the stool and led me to a small paved area with folding chairs and a small round table. "Tom and I sit up here in the evenings in the summer. Best view in town."

"Is Mr. Grayson here?"

"He's in his office downstairs."

"Is he still yelling at God?"

She smiled at me. "Yes, he is. But he's all right."

"I came because you invited me, and because I wanted to ask you . . . I wanted to talk to you."

"I'm glad." Mrs. Grayson rubbed at a splotch of blue paint on her thumb, like she was working up to something. "Evie, I read all about it in the paper. I think by the end I started to understand what was happening. You loved him, didn't you? I'm so sorry for your loss."

My loss.

Loss.

That's what it was, a hole I could never fill. It would be bottomless. I would have all the not knowing what happened to him, and beside it would be this loss. Never to see him again, never to see his walk or his smile. That was gone from the world forever.

The first time he kissed me it had been an impulse he regretted.

The second time he kissed me it had been a man to a woman. I wasn't too young. He wasn't too old. My mother hadn't existed for us. Everything had gone away except us.

There had been love between us at that moment. He had loved me, at that moment.

"Nobody ever said that to me," I told her. "Nobody ever said they were sorry. I hadn't even said it. Not even to myself. He's dead, isn't he?"

In Mrs. Grayson's eyes was the sadness I'd always seen. Now I had it, too.

"Yes, petal. He is."

He was dead, really dead. It was all gone, his beautiful forearms, his throat, his laugh.

I felt tears build up inside my chest, and even though I was good at pushing tears away, this was something I could not stop.

The first sob escaped, and I rocked forward, burying my face in my hands. I was embarrassed but I couldn't stop.

She waited. I could feel her sympathy. After a while I felt her get up and search through her pockets, then go over to her worktable. She came back and put a rag in my hands.

"It's clean," she said. "Barely."

I laughed, and she did, too. I wiped my face.

"Now, petal," she said. "Tell me why you came."

I told her about what Peter had told me, about the

fortune in the warehouse, about how Joe got his money. About halfway through, she got up and went to the ledge just a few paces away. I got up and joined her and kept talking while we looked out at the city. It was easier to talk when she wasn't looking.

"So I took the money that's left, the eight thousand dollars," I said. "Gladys brought it down for a bribe, but she didn't need it. I want to give it to you."

Mrs. Grayson swiveled and looked at me.

"You must know people who need it," I continued. "That friend — that family friend you know who was in the camps. And he must know people, and they must know people, and they must need money because everything was taken from them, and they can start over . . ."

"Evie, stop. I can't take this money."

"But you have to. It's the only way!"

"I can't take stolen money."

"It's nobody's money now. It's not Joe's. Would you rather he bought a house with it?"

"But it's not for me to say," Mrs. Grayson told me. "I'm not a judge, I'm not . . ." She waved her hands helplessly. "I'm not equipped for this."

"Then donate it somewhere. Just take it, because if you don't, we're doomed. The family. It's bad enough that I don't know," I said. "Don't you see, I don't *know* what happened on that boat. I don't know what kind of man Joe is. But I do know he did this one bad thing, at least. Peter said that somebody had to pay. Well, it can't be him. It just can't be. He might have been a thief and a liar and a cheat, but he was a good person."

Mrs. Grayson choked back a laugh. Then she stared down at the little suitcase, stared at it hard.

"I'll never tell Joe that I gave it to you," I said. "I promise."

"It's not that. What will he do to you?"

"Nothing. There's nothing he can do. He owes me too much."

Mrs. Grayson hugged herself, shaking her head helplessly.

"All the way back home, on the drive, I was thinking about penicillin," I said. "You know how they found it? The guy who found it was a slob. He kept his laboratory a mess, stuff everywhere — he'd leave it for weeks and months . . . and one day he finds a mold. It was an accident. Out of this mess, this *contamination*, comes . . ."

"Deliverance," Mrs. Grayson murmured.

"Deliverance," I said.

Back at home, it was time for Grandma Glad to get home from church. She would be walking up the stairs, holding on to the banister. She would go into her room and the first thing she would do was open the closet and look up at the shelf. I'd watched her do it yesterday — every time she came into her room she'd make sure it was there. Today, the shelf would be empty.

She would call for Joe, and he would come quick, alarmed at the tone in her voice. Mom would come, too, but they'd shut her out. Grandma Glad would talk about calling the police but Joe would say no. After maybe a minute or so, they'd think about me.

There would be hell to pay, but I was all right with that. I would pay that price. There was nothing they could do to me.

I swung down Forty-eighth and turned left on Sixth Avenue, heading away from my train. I felt light without the valise. I would walk for a while. The wind had kicked up, and it was blowing papers around like crazy. I looked down at my feet as I stepped on every crack. I didn't believe in bad omens anymore, or luck.

Dusk had fallen, and lights were coming on in all the apartments around me. Little squares of gold. I realized then that this was what Mrs. Grayson was painting, blue shadows and golden light. Behind every square of gold was a person. Maybe a family. How nice it must be to wake up and know so many busy lives were around you, in the humming hive of the city.

I felt something clear and straight inside me, and I knew I'd found home. I'd live here one day. I'd be in one of those golden squares of light. Around me would be a bunch of lives, some better, some worse. I'd be smack in the middle of all that living.

Joe would lose the money he'd counted on for his dream house. Mom and I weren't going anywhere. We would live in the house we hated, but that was okay, too, because maybe we were just getting a little bit of what we deserved.

What did I owe Peter? I knew the answer now. Something bigger than the truth. A little bit of justice — not for him, but for people he didn't even know.

During the war, whenever we had to give something up or put something off, we'd say it was "for the duration." Because we didn't know when the war would end, but we knew we'd stick with whatever we had to do.

So here I was. I would live with Joe and Mom. I had no place else to go. Joe would carve the roast on Sundays. He would put up the Christmas tree. They would hand me the phone, pick up my socks, leave the porch light on. I would never know what happened on the boat that day, but they would be my parents. For the duration.

But while I'd be their daughter, while I'd eat the roast and come home from dates and wash the dishes, I would also be myself. I would love my mother, but I would never want to be her again. I would never be what someone else wanted me to be. I would never laugh at a joke I didn't think was funny. I would never tell another lie. I would be the truth teller, starting today. That would probably be tough.

But I was tougher.

Acknowledgments

*A*cknowledgment is way too genteel a word for the buckets of gush I want to dunk on the heads of those in my life who aided and abetted this book. First off, my amazing editor, David Levithan, truly a hunk of heaven, who took me to lunch and listened to a coming-of-age story involving blackmail, adultery, and possible homicide and said, "Cool!" Thank you, dear D, for your support and "perfect plumb" (look it up) over lo these many years. And a hunka burning love to everyone at Scholastic who liked this book and worked for it.

My cowgirl hat is hereby swept off in homage to my posse, Elizabeth Partridge, Julie Downing, and Katherine Tillotson, all of whom chase away blues and Mean Barbara like nobody's business. I am indebted to Donna Tauscher, as always, for her support, insight, and grace; to Jane Mason, gentle soul, fierce ally, and a friend forever; and to Meredith Ziemba, for sharing her stories, similes, art supplies, and whatever else she has in her truck at any given moment.

Every writer who tackles the historical past ends up standing on the shoulders of those who wrote insightfully about the period. I am especially indebted to Jan Morris for her fine book, *Manhattan '45*, and to Kevin Coyne for *Marching Home*. For those interested in the story of the Gold Train and the strange journey that ended in an army warehouse in Salzburg, there are numerous Web sites with historical documents to peruse. For a definitive history, I relied on *The Gold Train*, by Ronald W. Zweig. The excellent research department at the *Palm Beach Post* sent me exhaustive accounts of the 1947 hurricane. A tip of the hat to Sandy Simon's charming *Remembering: A History of Florida's South Palm Beach County*. Kelli Marin and Kathleen Holmes, experts in all things Florida, helped me out with hurricane holes. It was a lucky day when I stumbled on Barbara Holland's memoir, *When All the World Was Young*. Her prose is so crystal-perfect that I have a strong desire to put on a fetching hat and buy her a cocktail at some swanky hotel bar. A special thank-you to my parents for sharing newspapers and memories and photographs of their own journeys in the postwar years, as well as giving me all the support and love I could ever wish for.

And now, I saved the best for last. A toast to you, Neil and Cleo: To the moon and back.

DATE DUE

JUN 1 1 20			
GAYLORD			PRINTED IN U.S.A.